THE DISMAL SWAMP

A BRANDON HALL MYSTERY

JOHN THEO JR.

Print Edition
Copyright © 2019 John Theo Jr.
All rights reserved.

Published in the United States by CKN Christian Publishing, an imprint of Wolfpack Publishing, Las Vegas.

CKN Christian Publishing
An Imprint of Wolfpack Publishing
6032 Wheat Penny Avenue
Las Vegas, NV 89122

christiankindlenews.com

Ebook ISBN 978-1-64119-732-8
Paperback ISBN 978-1-64119-733-5

In loving memory of Karl Karra.

THE DISMAL SWAMP

Matthew 18:6

"But whoso shall offend one of these little ones which believe in me, it were better for him that a millstone were hanged about his neck, and that he were drowned in the depth of the sea."

ONE

MY DAD HELD DOWN THE BULL CALF WITH BOTH HIS HANDS and a knee. I released the rubber loop from the bander. In about a week, the dead flesh would fall off. I nodded to Dad who let go of the calf. The animal got up and ran to his mother.

"No matter how old we are," Dad said, pointing to the calf, "we all want our momma when we're afraid."

"Sorry to make you into a eunuch fella," I said.

Behind us came sound of wood breaking. A moment later it was followed by shouting. My buddy, Colt Burnell, and his younger brother Moss, erected an arbor in front of our main pond. Both of the chubby bearded young men wore matching jean overalls. Colt stepped back to view the lopsided arbor before yelling at Moss.

My dad pointed to the brothers. "They gonna have that ready in time for the wedding?"

"I hope so. It's in three hours."

"I'm glad you offered the farm to Colt for his special day. The place needs this."

"You act like the farm's a living thing."

"It is." Dad waved his arm over to the recently hayed pastures and clear skies. "This property's too nice not to share. It needs life on it. Look around us, Son. We have the best job in the world."

It was nice to get a reminder of how blessed I was. There were times I second-guessed the choice to carry on the farm. Times when friends, who worked at fancy jobs in big cities, took their families on expensive vacations. I'd cringe every time Annie would open their gorgeous vacation pictures plastered on social media. She never complained, but I knew she'd welcome a week on the Outer Banks, or the Eastern Shore. I remembered the cost those friends paid for the fancy vacations. They were stuck in traffic jams and spending fifty plus hours a week in cubicles and cramped offices, missing time with family. I would never give my daughter a wealthy inheritance, but I would give her memories of growing up outdoors and spending time with her family.

Colt appeared at the fence line. "Brandon, I'm heading into the barn to get ready."

"You can use the shower in the house, you know."

"I'm good," he said. "Thanks again for letting Opal and me have our wedding here."

"My pleasure."

His dark-haired younger brother came up behind him. "I'll take you up on the shower if that's okay."

"There's an outdoor shower on the side of the barn," Colt said, clearly annoyed with his sibling.

"Mom didn't pack my flip flops with my lunch and it's dirty around the shower."

Colt shook his head. "I can't believe the stuff you say out loud, Moss. You're a twenty-one-year-old momma's boy."

Dad was trying not to laugh. I cut in. "Moss, go ahead and use our shower."

Colt grabbed his brother by his overalls and dragged him toward the barn. He called back to me, "My brother will be fine using the barn shower, thanks."

"I'll see you fellas at the altar in a few."

After they were out of range my dad said, "Those two remind me of Martin and Lewis."

"Yeah, but it's not an act."

Our natural path back to the house led us through the wrought iron gate into the family's ancestral cemetery. Ancient alabaster stones were juxtaposed with a single new thick grey headstone which read, *Jonah Hall, March 12, 2015-August 10, 2017. Beloved son and brother. Now resting in the arms of our Savior.* Much of my heart was buried in that red clay cemetery plot. It seemed like just yesterday that Annie's car was hit by a drunk driver along Route 501. Since then God had healed our brokenness, but there would always be a hole in my heart in the shape of my infant son.

We stopped in front of Jonah's headstone. "Sometimes it seems like I held him in my arms only yesterday," I said, "and other times it feels like it's been an eternity. Or worse, like it was a dream and he was never really here."

"He was here, Brandon." My dad placed one of his massive hands on my shoulder.

"I hate that life just goes on."

"I know."

A passage came to mind from the book of Job. Here was another man who suffered a loss greater than me. "The righteous also shall hold his way, and he that hath clean hands shall be stronger and stronger."

"Amen."

I turned to my Dad using every bit of self-control to

keep from crying in front of the tough man. "The problem is, I feel weaker and weaker."

"It's a paradox," he said. "In Corinthians it says that His strength is made perfect in weakness. For when I am weak —" he stopped, waiting for me.

"Then I am strong," I finished.

Dad put his arm around me and walked us back toward the farmhouse. It reminded me of the way I used to help my Marine buddies get home when we were overseas and they were drunk. I rarely drank alcohol and was always the designated chaperone. The muscular arm draped over my shoulder felt secure and gave me the false impression that Dad would always be there to look out for me. I was fast approaching forty years old and I still needed him. I would always need him. We reached the farmhouse and Dad finally let go. I felt like a heavy weight was placed back on my shoulders.

He got into his truck. "I'll be back in ten minutes with the package," he said.

I gave him a thumbs up. "Roger that."

He drove out the gravel driveway onto the street and made an immediate sharp left turn onto the parallel driveway which led to his log cabin hidden deep on the property.

I entered through the side screen door into the kitchen. The smell of coffee and bacon assaulted my senses. Annie stirred scrambled eggs in a cast iron skillet with her other hand resting on a baby bump that looked bigger than the day before.

I kissed her dark hair, then her full lips, then her belly. "How's little John Wayne Hall doing?"

"If the baby happens to be a boy," she said, picking a piece of grass out of my hair, "We're not naming him John Wayne Hall."

My eleven-year-old daughter Emily came downstairs still in her pajamas. She held up both a pink and a lavender dress. She was a spitting image of her mother with pale skin and smiley eyes. "Which one should I wear for the wedding?"

"The longer one," I said, pouring a cup of coffee.

Emily ignored me and looked to her mother who said, "The lavender."

"That's what I was thinking," Emily said.

"Yeah, the lavender one works," I chimed in, like I knew what I was talking about.

"You're so annoying," Emily said, turning to go back upstairs.

I put down the coffee mug, growled, and started up the stairs after her. "The tickle monster loves sleepy kids who are grouchy."

Emily laughed and ran up the remaining steps two at a time towards her bedroom. I changed my voice back to normal and shouted up the stairwell. "Let's have breakfast out on the porch."

It was May in Southern Virginia and the mornings were the perfect goldilocks temperature, not too hot nor too cold. Coupled with no mosquitos made it as close to perfect as we would find in this fallen world. The three of us brought our scrambled eggs and turkey bacon onto the porch and sat in rocking chairs. The view looked out over our piece of paradise. We owned five hundred acres in the small southern Virginia town of Nathalie. The farm went back a long way in my family, but no one ever thought to name it. When Annie and I took it over from my parents we named it, *Twenty-Three-One,* after the Psalm of the same number. *The Lord is my shepherd, I shall not want.* The Lord lived up to that promise during many tough times.

Five minutes later, Dad pulled up with Mom in the

passenger seat of the truck. They both got out and walked up to the porch. My mom looked like a child next to my dad's six foot three broad frame. I maxed out at five foot nine inches. My dad loved to prod me by saying I inherited two things from my mother: her height and her disposition. It was obvious the latter was a compliment with the former being a dig. At thirty-seven I was still in relatively good shape, but I'd still lose nine out of ten rounds with my fifty-eight-year-old father who still kept in shape from his days in the military. Emily hugged my mom and jumped into Dad's arms.

"I heard you were turning sixteen this week?" Dad said.

"Twelve," Emily corrected.

"Twelve, that's what I said."

Mom elbowed him gently. "Stop teasing your grand-daughter."

"We want to give you an early birthday present," Dad said. "Your old man and I drove all the way out to Danville to pick it up last week."

Emily started jumping up and down.

Annie turned to me. "What did you get?"

"Just something small," I said.

"What is it?" Emily said, continuing to jump up and down. "Tell me!"

"Grandpa, maybe we should wait for her actual birth-day," I said, teasing Emily.

"No, Daddy. That's mean."

"Oh, just give her to Emily," my mother said, walking back to the truck.

"Her?" Annie said, her head snapping in my direction.

I shrugged my shoulders and gave my best *aw shucks* grin I could muster. Suddenly, a black and white furry face popped up against the glass of the driver's side door of my dad's truck.

Emily screamed, "A puppy!"

"She's a collie," I said. "A great farm dog."

Dad opened the truck door and handed the puppy to Emily. She grabbed the puppy like she was a teddy bear and hugged her so tight the puppy squeaked.

"I love her."

"Easy," Dad said. "She's not a toy."

"And she's not cheap," I added.

Annie rolled her eyes before refocusing them on me like a laser. "I'm so glad you're happy, Emily. Your father and I had a lot of discussions about this." Sarcasm oozed from her statement.

"Sorry," I whispered. "I wanted to surprise you both."

"Oh, I'm surprised alright."

Emily rolled around in the grass with the puppy who proceeded to pee on her foot, but Emily didn't seem to care. When the puppy finished, I picked her up and placed the soft fluffy dog into my wife's lap. Annie gritted her teeth, trying desperately to fight against the onslaught of cuteness. The puppy started to lick her face. Within seconds my wife was defeated and held the puppy up against her face, kissing her head. After a minute I had to pry the dog from Annie so I could place her back onto the grass. Emily kept picking her up and kissing her. My parents took up occupancy in the two empty rocking chairs. I went inside and returned with a pitcher of sweet tea and mason jars. The four of us were content watching the two adorable dark-haired females frolicking in the grass.

"What are you going to name her?"

Emily picked up the puppy and looked her eye to eye. After a long pause she pulled a blade of grass from the puppy's mouth. "Fescue."

"Like the hay grass?"

"Yes," she said, placing the puppy back down. The dog started to eat more of the grass she was named after. "Fescue," she repeated.

As if to ruin my good mood, Annie leaned over to me. "Remember, you're coming to the homeschool conference."

"When and where is it again?"

"Don't play dumb, Brandon. I told you it's on Monday in Richmond."

"I hate the city."

"You need to come."

"I really don't want to leave the farm."

"This is your daughter's education we're talking about."

"Throw in some smoochie time later tonight."

"Brandon!"

My dad chuckled and my mom blushed.

Emily said, "Dad, I heard that!"

An hour later we stood on the porch as Dad snapped photos of the three of us dressed for the wedding. Annie wore a calico dress with her dark hair up in a bun. Em, wore her lavender dress with her hair in pigtails. Everyone laughed when I opened my mossy oak blazer to reveal matching mossy oak overalls. Colt and his brothers loved their overalls.

"Redneck chic," my dad said.

I snapped the overalls suspenders. "I'm the only non-family member in the wedding party so I guess this is an honor."

A short while later, a long line of old American-made pickup trucks entered our driveway. I stepped off the porch and approached the first truck. An elderly woman I recognized as Colt's grandmother rolled down the window, but it got stuck halfway. The petite woman tried to stand up.

"Hi Granny," I said, viewing the long line of pickups behind her. "That's quite a family you got there."

The proud matriarch said, "Where ya want the family to park?"

I pointed beyond the barn to where Colt's pickup was parked. "Park next to your grandson's truck."

"Thanks sweetie," she said.

The next truck had Colt's two other brothers, Wes and Wyn, in it. Their father had been a firearms buff and named all his boys after gun manufacturers. Colt, Wynchester with a Y, Wesson, and Mossberg were all only a year apart. They were true southern boys who loved Nascar, fishing, hunting, and even raced lawnmowers on weekends. You couldn't ask for more loyal friends. The brothers were both dressed like me with mossy oak overalls. I slung a thumb through my suspenders and raised my eyebrows to show off my matching attire. Wyn gave me a thumbs up.

Annie came alongside me to help welcome the parade of trucks. "With your beard you fit right in with those Burnell boys," she said, stroking my beard with one hand and patting my belly with the other.

I laughed and smacked my gut which had over the past few years gone from a six pack down to a four pack. "I'm not that, uhm, portly, am I?"

"Just more of you to love," Annie said with a wink.

I was happy her sense of humor was back. In the first few months after Jonah's death I was terrified of losing her. At one point she had withered to under a hundred pounds. It was a long time before she could function at a normal level, and longer still before her smile returned.

Emily came up alongside us, holding the puppy. "Can I bring Fescue?"

"I think we need to leave her on the porch," I said.

"Bring me the puppy," my dad said. "We're gonna sit on the porch and watch the wedding from here."

The wedding was held under a massive solitary oak in front of the main pond. Colt had met his fiancée, Opal, at the diesel repair shop they both worked at. Opal ran the front desk while Colt worked out back under the engines. Opal was a petite blonde who was overshadowed by Colt's large burly frame, but they seemed to fit together.

Throughout the ceremony Opal didn't stop smiling. When she looked at him, I could tell she didn't see a chubby bearded man, but a knight in shining armor. Colt was more reserved, but I could see the fire in his eyes every time he looked at her. Colt's pastor from Scottsburg performed the ceremony. When the brief service ended, Colt reached down and picked his petite bride off the ground to kiss her. He held her this way as people snapped photos. Opal didn't seem to care.

Colt's brothers had set up picnic tables and strung up lights on the backside of the barn. The farm had never looked so good. Each of Colt's brother's gave speeches while we waited in line for BBQ. The band was a local group that played both country-western and bluegrass music. We started with line dancing and mixed in two-step. Even pregnant, my wife moved with a grace that dwarfed my meager skills. At one point, granny put on a show of clogging all by herself. There had never been this many smiling people on the farm at one time. It was intoxicating. The sun was bright in the near cloudless sky and the view over the pastures and main pond was stunning.

The reception ran all afternoon. Early that evening, I danced one final time under the lights with Annie to the static of an AM radio while the band packed up. The place was empty of guests but the energy from the event still echoed throughout the farm. Colt and Opal kept thanking

Annie and me for letting them have the wedding on the farm. We, in turn, kept thanking them for letting us be a part of their ceremony and the memories they created on the property. It seemed like only yesterday that a horrific shootout had taken place on the farm and the new memories were a blessing that helped cover over the sins of the past.

TWO

THE NEXT DAY WAS SUNDAY. WE HAD AN EARLY BREAKFAST and met my parents at church. Dad taught an adult Sunday school class on the symbolism of wilderness in the Bible. He highlighted how many times Christ would go to the wilderness and mountains to pray. The outdoors held a special place for my dad and me. We hunted, fished, and made our livelihood from the land. Dad made sure to temper his enthusiasm for nature by quoting Romans one, stating that we are always to worship the Creator, not the creation. The rest of the day involved naps, reading, and a phenomenal dinner of steak and potatoes.

Monday morning I was up before dawn to drive the pastures. It was amazing how quick a mental to-do list filled my mind. A broken fence post here, water needed there, and an encroaching section of brambles near the woods needed to be brush-hogged. Back at home, Annie had coffee in a thermos and muffins packed in a basket. Emily was dressed, but clearly not awake.

"You sure we have to go to this homeschool thing?"

"The homeschool convention is once a year," Annie

said. "I already have Emily's curriculum set but want to sit in on one or two of the seminars on science." She handed me a piece of paper.

"What's this?"

"That's the seminar I want you and Emily to sit in on."

I read the sheet. "Math. Seriously?"

"I know you helped Emily with history last year, but once little John Wayne Hall comes along you might have to step up to do most of the primary teaching until I get back on my feet."

Emily laughed. I couldn't think of a witty comeback and just took the sheet and stuffed it into my pocket and tickled my daughter.

"Stop," she giggled. "You're so mean."

My dad showed up to grab Fescue. I felt weird leaving him alone to work the farm for the day. "You sure you don't need me here?" I said, hoping he'd pick up on my coded plea.

"I'll be fine. You go enjoy yourselves."

He knew how much I loathed the city and seemed to enjoy watching me squirm. We took Annie's Jeep as my old 1976 F250 pickup wouldn't make the two-plus hour drive north to Richmond. It was clear skies, with the temperature hovering around eighty with little traffic until we hit the city. We made good time and were there by 9:30 a.m.

The convention was held in an outdoor pavilion. It was a place where flea markets and farmers markets were held in the summer. An elderly man wearing a bow tie was at the entrance handing out pink and blue gift bags full of swag. Emily took a pink bag with a *thank you* and handed it to me. It was chock full of pens, pencils, rulers, and all sorts of homeschool knick-knacks. There were product sheets advertising the latest in homeschool software, hardware, books and teaching tools. At the bottom was a small teddy bear.

"Here," I said, giving her the teddy bear.

"No thanks," she said.

I held the teddy bear close to my chest as if I were offended. At what point did my baby girl stop liking stuffed animals? It was then I noticed something different about Emily's face.

"Are you wearing makeup?"

"Just lip gloss and some eyeliner."

I turned to Annie holding up the teddy bear. "She's not a baby," Annie said.

"I hate it," I said, licking my thumb and trying to wipe off some of her makeup.

"Stop," Emily said. "You're embarrassing me."

Annie cuffed my shoulder and gave me a stern, but somewhat comical, look. "Please don't embarrass us."

Before I could respond, someone smacked me in the rear. It was loud enough to draw attention from everyone in my immediate area. I turned to see my buddy JT oblivious to the stares of the patrons. He had on his beloved Red Sox baseball cap covering his balding head and wore a large grin.

"What's up, loosa?" he said in his thick Boston accent.

"What are you doing here?"

"I'm here with the ladies," he said, nodding towards one of the kiosks.

I scanned the crowd and picked up Sally Eldridge and her eight-year-old daughter Brooke who were talking with Annie and Emily.

"You got sucked into this convention too?"

"I don't mind," he said. "It's refreshing to be back in a city. I can feel its pulse."

"It's amazing how you feel that way towards lifeless

buildings while I feel suffocated being away from the farm."

"It's what makes the world go round, brotha."

JT had moved down to Halifax County from the hi-tech world of Boston, Massachusetts after his wife up and left him for his business partner. He literally threw a dart at a map and moved to southern Virginia to get out of the rat-race and away from a city, and job, he associated with pain and suffering. I met him at a local coffee shop when I accidentally cut him in line and he cussed me out. We somehow became friends and met for coffee on a regular basis. Through a series of events he became a believer and started attending our church. He met Sally almost a year ago and fell hard for her. She was a widower whose husband passed away in Afghanistan almost a decade earlier. It was nice to see a smile on my friend's face. He had been through a lot.

The two of us started to walk along the busy market. "JT, did you ever, in your wildest imagination, think you'd end up at a Christian homeschool event in Richmond Virginia?"

"Not in a million years, but it's a nice change from what I'm used to." He pointed to the clear sky. "Back home in Massachusetts it's still cold, yet here I am enjoying a beautiful spring day in Southern Virginia walking around in a short sleeve shirt."

"You seem awfully chipper today?"

He grinned and winked at me as if he were up to something.

We reconvened a short while later with the ladies. Annie and Sally went to the same science seminar while her daughter Brooke went to an art class. JT worked on a small laptop at a nearby bench. It was nice to see him embrace technology again. For a while he gave up on his high-tech background after his wife left him. Just like our ideas of city life versus country living, the thought of working on a computer was foreign to me. I could never see myself doing anything but farming. The scuba diving and P.I. work I did on the side could go away, but farming was a lifeline.

Emily and I went to the math seminar. The instructor was an older woman who spoke passionately about math and how it was one of the languages of God. She presented the material in such a way that I found it interesting. Math was something that I knew was necessary in life but never found attractive. The way this woman portrayed it was revolutionary. Math transcended language barriers and cultures. Everyone spoke the same language with math. Emily even seemed intrigued with the speaker, but still whispered that it was her least favorite subject.

From the main portion of the mall came the sound of a raised voice. Everyone in the seminar seemed unfazed. Maybe it was being in the city that had me on high alert, but something seemed off. A moment passed and the female voice turned into a loud cry for help. I tapped Emily's shoulder and she instinctively followed me. We exited into the main corridor of the open-air pavilion. The woman's voice turned into more cries. A crowd started to form twenty yards in front of us. I assumed someone was hurt. Possibly a heart attack, or someone passed out from the spring heat. I checked my phone and saw no texts from Annie. We approached the crowd and the woman's cries had now morphed into hysterical screams. A woman in her thirties was calling out for someone named Rebecca.

"Has anyone seen my daughter, Rebecca?" The empty faces staring back at her seemed to answer the question. She looked around and shouted again, "Rebecca!"

My phone text pinged. It was Annie asking where

Emily and I were and what the commotion was? I texted that we were fine.

A chubby security officer forced his way through the crowd. He spoke into a walkie talkie clipped to his shoulder. He finished saying something then turned to the crying woman. "When did you last see her?"

The woman's eyes were crazed. "Uhm, ten minutes ago. I've been looking for ten minutes," she repeated.

The security officer spoke into his walkie talkie again. "Activate Code Adam."

I knew the procedure was named after Adam Walsh, the six-year-old son of John Walsh who was abducted and murdered back in 1981. Adam's dad, John, went on to become a famous television personality advocating for child safety. Per the Code Adam, security officers started to appear at all the exits. Being outdoors, these exits were nothing more than brick walkways. Anyone could leave the area by stepping over mulch beds and bushes. The place was a porous, unsecured nightmare. The security officer in front of me had the woman give him all the statistics of her daughter, Rebecca.

"She's nine-years-old, has long blonde hair with pale skin and dimples," the mother said, clearly trying to focus. "She's tall for her age, wearing a pink top, and uhm, denim skirt and pink cowboy boots."

She described a blonde version of my daughter. My heart ached for this woman. I would never wish this on my worst enemy.

Emily started to cry. "Daddy? Is the girl okay?"

"I don't know baby," I said, pulling her off to the side away from the chaos.

Annie found us. We all gave each other a group hug. After I explained what was happening, I said, "This is why I always tell you guys to have situational awareness. I hope the girl just is lost."

Emily continued to cry with Annie joining in. "Oh, that poor woman."

The three of us created a tight circle and started to pray for the young girl named Rebecca whom we had never met. The moment we finished praying there was another shout followed by many shouts, and then a crash. In the distance a tall kiosk banner collapsed as two men wrestled on the ground. Security descended on the area. Behind us the sounds of sirens from local PD added to the circus of noise. The security guard standing with the woman spoke into his walkie talkie.

After a long pause a crackling voice called back on the radio, "I think we found the girl. We're down at the bathrooms."

"Make way," the security guard yelled, pushing through the crowd and half dragging the mother towards the bathrooms.

We, along with about twenty other people, followed the crowd down past an exit to where the bathrooms were located. A security guard had his knee in the back of a young man lying face down on the ground in handcuffs. He was skinny to the point of being emaciated with a bald head with long ponytail in the back. Another officer brought over a young girl with short blonde hair to the hysterical woman. The girl was stoic, in direct contrast to her mom's sobbing.

She pulled the girl in and hugged her before she pushed her to her arm's length. "What did he do to you?"

One of the security guards said, "He had already changed her coat and cut her hair. It was the pink cowboy boots that I picked up on."

"Oh thank you, thank you." She turned to the handcuffed man on the ground and screamed. "You sick demon. What is wrong with you?"

He didn't respond. Two police officers pulled him upright. They led him past the crowd where he revealed no emotion. Everyone who looked at the man seemed disgusted. A few men were being held back by security officers who wanted to exact some form of justice on the guy. More police showed up. It was then I noticed that some of the patrons even had their cell phones out taking a video. It was a sad reminder of the strange world we lived in.

Annie, Emily, and I walked over to the nearest bench and sat down. We prayed again, thanking God for rescuing the little girl. The knot in my stomach started to untie itself.

"I think I had enough excitement for one day," I said. "I want to go home."

"But we just got here," Annie said.

Emily echoed my thoughts. "I want to go back to the farm, Mom. I'm really freaked out."

Annie paused, "Okay, but I'd like to grab one or two pamphlets from some vendors on the way out. I guess I can look the rest of the information up online."

"I'll get the Jeep and meet you at the entrance," I said. "Emily, you're with me."

Before we could leave another shout rose above the commotion. The knot in my stomach rewound itself. I pulled Emily close and my hand dropped under my shirt to rest on the appendix holster holding my Smith and Wesson nine-millimeter handgun. The female shout turned into screams. It was coming from beyond the bathrooms from the area that we had just left. I wandered back over to see what the problem was this time. A crowd started to form around another woman. It was Sally. She was on her knees shouting for Brooke. JT stood over her, dumbfounded.

"JT, talk to me?"

"It's Brooke. We can't find her."

The same chubby security guard rushed over panting. He spoke into his microphone again. I heard him say the words, "Another missing child?" He knelt down next to Sally. "When did you see her last?"

"I don't know. After seeing what just happened, I rushed to get her at the art seminar and she's nowhere."

"What was she wearing?"

"I… I don't remember."

The guard spoke into his radio again, "Keep the Code Adam in place. I repeat, keep the Code Adam in place. We got another missing child."

Annie came up behind me with Emily. She saw Sally on the ground. "Dear Lord, no." She pushed me aside and knelt down beside her friend. They both started to pray.

Emily gripped my free hand like it was a lifeline keeping her from being washed away into the sea. Annie and Sally were bawling, and JT started to cry. I had only felt this hopeless one other time in my life. A time when my infant son was taken from me. Images of Jonah's lifeless, bruised body assaulted my consciousness. I dragged Emily away from the crowd and sat her down on a nearby bench.

"Sit here," I said.

"Don't leave me," Emily pleaded.

"I'm not," I said leaning over the bench pretending to spit into a boxwood shrub. The reality was that I felt like I was going to vomit. I coughed some and felt Emily's hand start to rub my back. I started to choke up. "I'm sorry baby. My heart is breaking right now. I keep thinking of your baby brother."

"It's okay Daddy," Emily said, wrapping a petite arm around me like a mother caring for a sick child.

I spit again to make sure I was okay before I turned back around. More police than I ever knew existed stormed the area. No one was allowed to leave. News reporters started to show up as well. I didn't let go of Emily's hand. Ten minutes later Annie came over to the bench with a tear-streaked face. She sat down next to us.

"She's gone, Brandon. Brooke's gone!"

"You sure it's not—"

Annie cut me off, "Cops have scoured the place. They're confident it was a coordinated abduction. They've never seen, or heard, anything like this happening before. FBI is on the way. I want you to take Emily home. I'm going to stay with Sally and JT."

"Are you sure?"

"Sally's a mess. I can't leave her."

I reluctantly agreed to my wife's proposal. I knew Annie would be safe with police everywhere. Still, I wanted to retreat back to the quiet, safe life on the farm as a family. We prayed together one more time.

I kissed Annie on the lips with a new appreciation. "Two things," I said. "I love you and be safe."

"Love you too."

I walked her back over to Sally and JT who were surrounded by police at this point. Sally held her stomach like her appendix had just burst, but I knew it was her heart that was broken. I felt sick over what just happened, and like an emotional coward, I kept from making eye contact. Some sinful part of me wished I had never known her so I wouldn't have to share in the horror and pain she was going through. An arm grabbed me. I turned to see JT who was a disheveled mess.

"Brandon, promise me you're gonna take this up."

"Police are on it and the FBI will get involved and—"

"I don't know them. I know you. I trust you only." It was as if JT could see my mind racing. As if he could tell I was trying to think up an excuse not to get involved. "You're a P.I. and can help. Where I come from loyalty is everything." After a pause he added, "If money's an issue—"

I held up my hand. "There's no way I'm taking your money. I'll do whatever you ask." JT exhaled as if I had already found Brooke. His confidence in me was intimidating. "JT, listen to me. I want you to sit with the Police and FBI when they get here. Give them everything they ask for. They have the resources that I don't. You give them everything they ask for," I repeated.

"Will do."

"At the same time, I want you to record all interviews on your phone."

"Understood."

"They won't let me sit in on the debrief as I'm not family, but the second you finish with them I want you to text me the recording."

JT nodded.

"I'm taking Emily back to the farm," I said. "Make sure you text me everything."

"Absolutely."

"I'll be praying for you guys."

A moment later everyone's phone went off with the same sickening sound. The morbid alert was activated by local government to warn citizens about flash floods, tornados, and child abductions called Amber Alerts. The criteria for an Amber Alert usually included the description of a perp and their vehicle. This was the first time I'd seen an Amber Alert with only the description of the missing child. Brooke's familiar stats crept over my cell phone stating the area of Richmond she was last seen.

At the exit I was stopped by an officer inspecting anyone trying to leave with small children. I showed him my license, and Emily showed her library card which had a picture on it to prove we belonged together. Once outside, I held Emily's hand all the way back to the Jeep.

THREE

The traffic out of the city was slow. We stopped for lunch at a Greek restaurant on the south side of Richmond, but neither of us seemed to have an appetite.

"C'mon," I said, pointing to Emily's salad with grilled chicken. "We both need to keep up our strength."

She started crying. The delay, and shock, of what happened had finally hit her. I got up and sat down beside her on the other side of the booth and held her tight, not wanting to let go. Over the years I had seen my daughter cry due to a variety of things. From an ankle sprain, to nightmares, to just being sad when I had to put a calf down, but these tears were different. It was a new arrow that had been placed in Emily's quiver of painful life experiences. It was wrong that she had to witness this at her age, but it was part-and-parcel of living in a fallen world. It was nothing compared to what Sally and Brooke were going through. I didn't know how to comfort my daughter and started to tear up as well. An elderly black woman sitting across from us watched with a sympathetic expression. It was as if she knew what we were upset over.

"I'm okay, Daddy," Emily said.

"We gotta have faith, sweetie. Even in this nightmare we must remember God is still in control."

"But how could He let this happen?"

"He didn't want this to happen, but man is a sinful creature full of wickedness and capable of great evil." I wasn't sure if she understood, so I added. "But He can take this situation and turn it around. I've seen it happen."

"When?"

"Remember when our septic system broke and Mommy and I were worried about how we'd pay for it?" She nodded. "And remember when those bad men came to our house?" She nodded again. "The broken septic system created a muddy yard during a drought, and God used the muddy yard to stop their truck from getting close enough to our house to hurt us."

"So how can He turn this situation around?"

My daughter stumped me. I had no idea how God could redeem this situation. For all I knew Brooke was already with Him in heaven due to some horrific act by her captor.

Kids had a great truth radar and so I answered honestly. "I don't know, sweetie."

Emily seemed to approve of my humble answer and started to eat. We finished our salads and I got a cup of coffee and each of us a cookie for dessert.

"On a side note," I said, biting into the cookie. "You've got to always have-"

"Situational awareness," she said in a mocking tone confirming how many times I had said this to her.

"Okay smarty-pants," I said. "Without looking up tell me how many people are in this restaurant."

"Uhm, I'm not sure."

"Twelve," I said. "Where's the nearest exit?" She turned around to look. "No cheating," I said.

"I'm not sure."

I pointed. "It's down the hallway behind us. You didn't realize, but I chose this booth as it faced the entrance and was near the rear exit. This way we can see who's entering and, in case of an emergency, we're near an exit to leave quick."

"Dad, don't be paranoid."

"I'm not. I learned this stuff in the military and it helped keep me safe overseas."

"We aren't in the military or overseas."

"So we're safe?" I said.

"No, I meant-"

"Did you know JT was at the 2013 Boston Marathon bombing. He watched people get blown apart." Normally this is where Annie would jump in and tell me to take it down a notch, but my wife wasn't here. I could see Emily was getting nervous, so I finished with, "I don't want you to go through life scared. Just promise me you'll have situational awareness and don't let strangers chat you up."

"But doesn't the Bible say to be kind to strangers because they could be angels?"

"Where in the world did you pull that from?"

"Youth group."

She was right, and I had to think for a moment before responding to the passage from the book of Hebrews. "You definitely got your mom's brain," I said.

She smiled even though her eyes still had tears in them. It was a strange contrast to observe. I seemed to be fighting a monster named sadness. I had fought this creature long ago when Annie grieved about the loss of Jonah. She withered away to the point of almost no return. During that time, I did everything possible to get her to eat, and even smile.

"The Bible also talks a lot about prudence and wisdom," I said. "And it also says to test all things, so ha."

The elderly woman sitting across from us got up and hobbled over with a cane. "I'm so sorry to interrupt," she said. "But are you two okay?"

I nodded and wiped my face to make sure I didn't look like a wreck. "A good friend of ours just had her child go missing and we're concerned."

She started to tear up. "Is this the child I heard about on the news a little while ago?"

"Yes, ma'am."

"Heartbreaking."

Emily cleared her throat. "Ma'am?"

"Yes, child?"

"Who do you say that Jesus is?"

The woman smiled, looked up, and rested her hand over her heart. After a moment she almost shouted. "He is the only Son of God, and my Lord and savior."

I felt like I was in church and felt obligated to add an *Amen* to her testimony.

"May God bless you both," she said. "I'll be praying for this child."

As the elderly woman walked out of the restaurant Emily whispered to me, "Do you think she was an angel?"

"You never know, sweetie. C'mon, we're almost out of the city and I can't wait to get back to the farm where I can breathe easier." Outside it was low eighties with very little humidity. Light grey clouds were blocking the sun, but we weren't scheduled for rain. "What do you think about taking the soft-top down on the Jeep?"

"Yes!" Emily shouted, giving me the excited response I had hoped.

The warm breeze was perfect for driving in the Jeep. I reached in the backseat and grabbed a ball cap for Emily. With her light skin she'd easily get a sunburn driving with the top down. At the next traffic light, I took my cell out of my pocket to place in a cup holder. My stockman pocket knife fell out as well. The pocket knife was given to me by my father when I was eight. I had this romantic notion of handing it down to my son when he was older, but God had other plans. Unless Annie had a boy, the family name was going to end with me. I looked over at Emily, staring out the window at a statue on a street corner. I was okay with her carrying on the family line, even if it meant our name would end. I was more than okay with it. A family, not a family name, were what mattered. In that category I was deeply blessed.

"Here," I said, handing the heirloom over to her.

"You're giving me your pocket knife?" She said. "The one grandpa gave you?"

"It's time you had one of your own. It's not a weapon or toy, but a tool."

"But—"

The light turned green and I started driving again. "I was planning on giving it to you on your birthday."

She held the stag-handled knife in her hand like it was precious gold. "But I always thought you were gonna give it to Jonah."

"He's not here, sweetie."

"What if Mommy has a boy though? Won't he want it?"

"And what if she does have a boy, and he doesn't want to be a farmer? You told me that you might want to be a farmer one day. If so, you'll need this."

"But what if I want to be a farmer's wife?" she said, as if she knew what I'd say in return.

"Won't happen."

She smiled, her dimples showing. "Why's that?"

"Cause Daddy ain't ever gonna let you date."

We both laughed.

"But what are you gonna do for a pocket knife? You use this all the time."

"I'll get another one."

I thought back over the past few years. The world had grown dangerous. Not so long ago there had been a shoot-out on my farm from a case I had worked on. A gentle-man's slip-joint pocket knife was a tool for a more civilized time. I needed something that was not just a tool but, if needed, a weapon.

Back at home we picked up Fescue at my parents. I gave them the debrief on what happened in Richmond while Emily played outside with her puppy. Mom and Dad knew Sally and Brooke Eldridge from church and were horrified.

My dad walked me outside, "I take it you're gonna try to help with the investigation?"

"FBI is all over this-"

"That's not what I asked."

I huffed. "I told JT that I'd do what I can."

"I'll pick up the slack here if you need to take time off from the farm. You get on this, son."

"Yes."

"Remember, the government is fat, slow, and nearly useless today. Your friends need you."

Up until that moment I had been trying to think of ways to stay out of the case, but he was right. The FBI agents assigned would go to bed each night leaving Brooke's case at work. Even if they loved their jobs, the case was still just a name on a piece of paper to them. I had to do something. As if in response to my decision, the phone pinged. It was a text from JT with an mp3 attached. It was the interview with the FBI.

I turned to my father. "Dad, can I leave Emily for a bit?"

"Of course."

"Thanks. Just bring her home at dinner time."

Somehow, I felt safer when Emily was at my parent's house. Maybe it was due to the shootout we had at the farmhouse? I liked that my dad's cabin was buried deep on the property. It was like a cozy hidden log cabin duck blind. No one could find it unless they looked real close. Back at the house, I sat on a porch rocking chair with a cup of sweet tea and pad of paper and listened to the voice recording from JT.

It was a bit muffled as JT had clearly hidden the phone in his pocket as he and Sally spoke with the FBI agents who identified themselves as part of the Child Abduction Rapid Deployment team, or CARD. Sally sniffled the entire time, interspersed with moments of weeping. One of the agents pushed back on the presence of JT, pointing out that he had no relation to Sally. I heard a scratching on the phone as JT reached into his pocket.

"I planned on remedying that tonight at dinner," he said.

"Oh, it's beautiful," Came Annie's voice.

"I'll permit him to stay if it's okay with you, Miss Eldridge?"

"Yes, please."

"Mrs. Hall will need to leave though."

I heard Annie's voice say something muffled before a door opened and closed.

The interview was almost an hour long and went from the mundane to the specific. They started with Brooke's description: eight years old, dirty blonde hair, blue eyes, fifty inches, thin, and pretty. The agents asked for clear spellings of names of anyone Sally had contact with, from family, to church, to stores they frequented back in Halifax

County. Brooke was homeschooled, which severely limited her interactions with people outside of the family.

Sally was born and raised in Southern Virginia and was an only child. JT was a transplant from Boston, Massachusetts with no siblings as well. Both Sally and JT's parents were deceased; however, Sally did have extended family throughout Virginia and North Carolina. The particular list was long. Sally was also part of several co-ops where she interacted with other homeschool families. These were groups where kids could learn specific skills they might not be able to learn at home, or online. Things such as art and music along with hands-on science experiments. Another long list of names and phone numbers followed. At this point Sally kept moaning and could barely respond to the questions. JT provided passwords to both of their emails and social media sites. JT offered his services as a programmer, but the agents assured him they had the resources to deal with the case.

I wrote down everything. JT kept pushing back on the agents, trying to gauge their thoughts on how soon they could recover Brooke, but they were keeping things close to the chest.

After several minutes of his pestering, a female agent said, "Based on initial data, these two abductions seemed coordinated and pre-planned, but the children they took were random as both families claim they don't know each other."

JT pressed them on this. "I don't mean to be rude, but I need someone to translate what you're saying into English."

A male agent said, "The abduction took place at an outdoor venue with no surveillance cameras. Tactically, it was the perfect target which leads us to believe this was premeditated. As to why they chose these two girls, we can't say. The sooner we can get the man in custody to reveal who he was working with the better. That's the best lead we have right now."

I kept the mp3 recording on the phone and looked down at the pad of paper in front of me. The majority of my private investigating work was insurance fraud. I had never worked on something even close to a missing persons case, but one thing I did know was that every second that went by the chances of finding Brooke dwindled. I stepped off the porch and walked over to the barn. For the next fifteen minutes, I busied myself cleaning out a stall for my dad's horse, Savannah. He kept her most days at his cabin, but she had a vacation condo in my barn when needed. I ran the interview over in my mind as I did the mundane chore, but nothing jumped out at me.

I had converted another one of the barn stalls into a small office and settled in to get caught up on paperwork. The life of a farmer in Southern Virginia wasn't glamorous or very profitable, but I still thought of it as romantic. Somehow each month we made our bills. Like the loaves and the fishes miracles from the Bible, God always provided for us.

The next stall I had converted into a small gym. I changed into sweats and sneakers and started with stretches before moving onto pull-ups, push-ups and crunches. As I ran on an old treadmill, I replayed the recording on speakerphone. The only thing that stuck was the guy they had in custody. His name was William Jeffers, and he was the key to unlocking everything. If the FBI could get him to reveal who he was working with then the case was all but solved. The entire time I kept waiting for my phone to ring and to hear JT say the FBI had found Brooke safe, but no call came. After two miles on the treadmill my body reminded me it was time for stretches again.

By the time I exited the barn, Dad and Emily were back. He stood over her near the porch, watching as she grilled chicken on the charcoal grill. He was explaining how important the marinade was.

"Smells great," I said.

"She's a natural," my dad said.

A newer diesel truck pulled into the driveway and stopped near the porch. I walked out to find Annie sitting in the passenger seat. Sarah, a friend from church, was in the driver's seat. They both look like they'd been crying.

Annie got out and hugged me. She pointed to Sarah. "This lady drove all the way up to Richmond to be there for Sally and ended up driving me home."

I leaned into the passenger window. "I can't thank you enough for bringing Annie home."

"You guys and Sally are like family and have been there for me during some tough times," Sarah started to say something else but could only get out Brooke's name before breaking down. She waved goodbye and backed out of the driveway.

I invited Dad to stay for dinner, but he declined, stating he had a date with his wife. The three of us barely ate that night. The only one who seemed to be happy and hungry was the puppy playing in the yard. Fescue chased anything that moved, be it squirrel or insect. I pressured Annie into eating a small piece of chicken by reminding her of the precious cargo she carried in her belly. A short while later Emily went in to watch an old movie leaving the two of us to sit out on the porch. The nighttime noise of chirping wildlife was a soothing soundtrack to the glittering stars above.

Now that we were alone, I said, "How's Sally holding up?"

Annie started to say something then broke down. I knelt down in front of her rocking chair. "It's okay, baby. Let it out."

"I feel so bad for Sally," she wept. "Her child is somewhere right now scared to death. I keep feeling like I'm going to be sick when I think this could have been Emily."

"I know this sounds harsh, but it wasn't Emily."

Annie broke down further. "This is horrific, Brandon."

"I know. I told JT I'm gonna do what I can from my end. He sent me an audio copy of the interview with the FBI."

"And?"

"Only real lead we have is the guy they have in custody. Clearly he was working with someone else. They need to get him to talk." I helped Annie off the rocking chair. "Come on."

In the living room Emily had on the movie *Roman Holiday* with Audrey Hepburn. The two of us joined her on the couch. An old fashion movie, devoid of violence and foul language, was a welcomed distraction.

FOUR

THE NEXT MORNING ANNIE AND EMILY ACCOMPANIED ME TO
the local farm supply store in downtown Halifax. I needed
to replace a couple of grease fittings on one of the tractors.
Whenever I went into town the girls always found an
excuse to come along so they could shop at the local stores.
In the back seat of the truck Fescue kept jumping around
while Emily was trying to read a book. The way Emily
scolded her sounded just like Annie.

"No, you listen," Emily said to the puppy. "You behave
or you're gonna get a time-out, you hear?"

I turned to my wife and picked up her hand. "Apple
doesn't fall far from the tree."

"So cute," Annie whispered.

At the farm supply store, Annie wandered into the
greenhouse to look for some herbs to plant in the garden.
Emily placed Fescue in the bed of the pickup before she
wandered the front of the store looking at a new pair of
cowboy boots. I found the grease fittings and stopped at a
glass display case next to the cash register. It was filled
with pocket knives.

Jessica, the middle age co-owner, stood behind the cash register. "See anything you like, Brandon?"

I pointed to a larger folding liner locking knife. "How much is this beauty?"

"Let me look it up," she said, typing on a computer.

The knife had a single large carbon steel blade, but had stag scales like my old knife, which gave it an old-school gentleman's feel. It also had a thumb stud to allow for quick opening with one hand.

"Sixty-five." I whistled, and she added "It's American made though."

"I know I'll use it so add it in."

I placed the grease fittings on the counter and took out my wallet. As if the sight of my credit card were a starting flag at a racetrack, Annie and Emily both appeared out of nowhere with items in hand. Annie placed a tray of cilantro and parsley on the counter. Emily placed a straw cowboy hat next to the herbs.

"I just came for a couple of grease fittings," I said. "I wasn't planning on buying the store out. We are on a budget you know."

Before Annie or Emily could give me a sales pitch on their items Jessica handed me the knife in a fancy box. "Here's your new knife Brandon."

Annie crossed her arms and gave me a huff. Emily mimicked her mother's actions. I grinned before turning to Jessica. "Might as well add their stuff in too."

Before returning home, we stopped at a coffee shop and walked a few of the stores in downtown Halifax. Each of us signed a book out of the town library. I chose a western, Emily picked up an old Nancy Drew mystery, and Annie chose a historical fiction set in her favorite era, the 1920s.

The girls wanted to look for a romance DVD in the

movie rental section of the library so I retreated to the truck. A text showed up on my phone. It was from Greg Schilling, a four term Virginia Senator and former client. He was going to be at his family estate in Clarkesville for the next ten days and said he would like to catch up. I texted back telling him that I'd make a point to stop by before he headed back to Washington.

On the drive home Annie said, "What's the plan?"

"I have some fences to work on and I want to get ahead of the summer by installing a new well, and—"

"That's not what I mean, Brandon. What are you gonna do about Brooke?"

I shrugged. "I'm not sure what I can offer, sweetie. The FBI does this for a living. My hope is the guy they have in custody will break down and give up the info they need. I'm sure he's being offered some sweet deals to talk about whomever he was working with."

"You keep saying that."

"You have another thought?"

"What if it was a coincidence?"

"No way," I said. "You know how I feel about coincidences."

"No such thing," she said, completing my thought.

On Mountain Road we saw a familiar black 1995 F350 speed past us in the opposite direction. It took a moment for me to recognize it as my dad's.

"Was that Grampy?" Emily said from the back seat.

I had already picked up my phone and handed it to Annie. "Call Dad to make sure he's okay? He was going awfully fast."

Annie left it on speakerphone, but it went to voicemail. She tried my mother's cell phone with the same response. I turned the truck around and gunned it.

"Daddy, is Grampy okay?" Emily said.

"I hope so, sweetie."

I caught up to Dad as he turned onto route 501. As we followed him south my gut tightened. Somehow, I knew where he was heading. Five minutes later we pulled into the Halifax Regional Hospital right behind him. His old truck pulled up to the Emergency entrance followed by my older truck.

"What's wrong, Dad?" I shouted, getting out of my truck.

My dad rushed to the passenger door. "Your mom's in a tremendous amount of pain. I had to lift her into the truck."

I heard her moan in the background. She was tough and I knew something was wrong for her even to make a noise. Without a word, Annie jumped into the driver's seat of my truck and pulled away to find a parking spot.

I grasped her hand. "Mom?"

A forced smile appeared on her face. "My baby," she said. "I don't want you to worry."

"Only you would think about me at a time like this," I said, more upset than I thought I should be.

An orderly came out with a wheelchair. My dad and I grasped hands under Mom's legs and lifted her from the truck into the chair. She shouted like we had just stabbed her. I had never heard Mom cry out in pain like this before.

My dad turned to the orderly. "My wife can't move. I think she has a pinched nerve in her back or something."

The orderly pointed to the Emergency room. "Go inside and get the paperwork started. I'll take your wife inside."

Annie and Emily came up alongside us. My mom forced another smile when Emily kissed her head.

"You okay?" Emily said.

"Your grampy thinks I just have a pinched nerve is all, sweetie. Hurts like the dickens though."

When we got inside my father was explaining Mom's symptoms to the receptionist. I left to go sit with Mom, Annie and Emily.

Dad came over when he finished checking her in. He picked up Mom's hand which all but disappeared in his large palm. "Brandon, your mother's been in pain for over a week and is just telling me now." He kissed her hand. "You're one stubborn woman."

My mom rolled her eyes as if to say, *you are far worse.* Her eyes closed and she seemed at peace for the moment. An orderly came out and told my father they were taking Mom back to get x-rays.

As Mom was wheeled away Dad said, "You should go check on the farm. There's nothing you can do here."

"You're kidding right?"

"I have a feeling it's gonna be a long day, Son." Before I could rebuke him, he whispered, "I don't have a good feeling about this."

"It's probably a pinched nerve like you said. Since she had her knee replaced, she's been pushing herself too hard."

"Maybe so," he said, walking away to go catch up with the orderly and Mom.

I turned to Emily and Annie. "I'm gonna take you guys home then come back."

"Are you sure?" Annie said. "I feel like we should all be here."

"Depending on how busy it is, Mom might not get seen for a while."

Annie slipped her hand into mine and we started walking back out to the truck. With my free hand I grasped Emily's outstretched hand.

On the drive home I could see that Annie was shaken up. I reached out and held her hand. "You okay?"

"This is too much," she said, referring to Mom's health and Brooke's abduction.

"I know," I said, but could not think of anything else to say that was comforting.

It was Emily who came up with comforting words from Psalm forty-six. "God is our refuge and strength, a very present help in trouble."

I looked over at my wife. "Your daughter is wise beyond her years."

At home I grabbed an apple and a bottle of water. My final words to Annie and Emily were asking them to keep praying for Mom. Maybe it was my dad's somber mood, but I was concerned. It seemed like a dark angel was hovering over the citizens of Halifax County as of late. I longed for sunshine, farming, and quiet peaceful nights on the porch.

Back at the hospital, I found Dad and Mom in a single room on the second floor. My dad motioned for me to step into the hall.

He whispered, "She's resting." The look of concern on my face asked a dozen questions. "They found something."

"Define something."

"A mass on her left kidney."

"Define mass."

"More than likely a tumor." The word was not always synonymous with cancer but had the same gut-punch effect. "There's a chance it could be benign but they're gonna confirm with another scan and then biopsy tomorrow morning. If it is malignant, they'll do a PET scan to see if it spread."

I sat down on the shiny white VCT floor. "I can't believe it."

My dad remained stoic. He started walking down the hall. I got up and followed.

"What do you need?" I said, struggling to keep up with his long strides.

"Prayer, lots of it." He stopped at a window and looked left and right like a trapped animal. "I need to get outside to some fresh air."

"C'mon, the stairs are this way."

Once outside, we walked around the building until we found a bench overlooking route 501. I could hear him taking in deep breaths and exhaling as if he were having a panic attack and trying to calm down. He had spent years in the military, and I knew first-hand he wasn't afraid of danger to himself. This time he fought an enemy most soldiers weren't used to. Cancer was a silent enemy they couldn't shoot, kill, or wrestle in their favor. It was torture when a warrior couldn't physically protect someone they loved.

"You okay?"

"Not really," he said.

"Sorry, that was a dumb question."

He rested his hand on my shoulder. "Thanks for being my son."

The compliment caught me off guard. Dad expressed his love for me in volumes of actions, but rarely in words. We stayed outside for almost a half hour, not saying much more. Back inside Mom was still resting. I kissed her on the forehead and went into the waiting area.

My cell had two missed phone calls, one from Annie and another missed call from a number in the Washington D.C. area. Annie didn't leave a voicemail, but the D.C. caller did.

"Brandon, it's Roger Drake calling. Your handsome

friend from Washington. I want to confirm we're still on for fishing this week."

My friend Drake was a special government agent and fellow believer. He came into my life through a series of random incidents culminating in a shootout on my property where he arrived just in time to save my skin. Since then, we had become fast friends trying to catch up whenever he had a break from his government work.

I called back and Drake picked up on the first ring. "Brandon, how's my brotha from anotha mutha doing?"

"How you stay upbeat in your line of work is nothing short of a mystery."

"The joy of the Lord, my man."

"About fishing," I said. "I'm not sure I can make it this week."

"If the James River is too far for you to travel, I can drive farther south to be closer to you-"

"That's not it." I proceeded to detail where I was, and why I was there. I also updated him on Brooke Eldridge.

When I finished he whistled. "I'm so sorry for what you're all going through. Tell me how I can help."

"Besides prayer, do you have enough clout to stick your nose into this missing person's case?"

"Not directly, but I can peek in from the background," he said. "I take it you're working on the case from your end?"

"Trying."

"First missing persons case?"

"Yeah."

"Let me give you some baseline info."

"Shoot."

"A child goes missing every minute in the US. In most child abductions, the abductors are usually family or close acquaintances, with a smaller percentage being strangers. Most of them are custody disputes. However, you told me Ms. Eldridge is widowed and has very few kin?"

"Correct."

"Then the FBI would normally be focusing on acquaintances of the family, but this whole double abduction attempt throws a wrench into the mix. It seems coordinated, so they'll be focusing on the guy they have in custody. Maybe it's some weird network?"

"Makes sense," I said, "but what's the motive if it's not a family member taking Brooke over a custody dispute?"

"It could be for a variety of reasons, none of which are good. Smuggling the children out of the country to sell. Did you know that human trafficking is the third largest international crime industry..." He paused as if to add weight to what he would say next. "In the world?"

"What are the first two?"

"Illegal drugs and arms running." I was speechless. I had no idea how pervasive this industry was. Drake continued, "Abductions could also be for other things such as the thrill of it, sex acts, and even black magic."

"What do you mean, black magic? Like child sacrifice?"

"That pagan stuff still exists, and it's on the rise."

It made me both furious and sick to think of all the children separated from their parents and their childhood's being ripped away. "So out of the reasons you listed, where do you think Brooke Eldridge falls?"

"I saw the picture of her on television. She's a pretty girl."

"And?"

"And I don't need to tell you which of the reasons the pervert probably had in mind when he abducted her."

"Lord help us."

There was a long pause before Drake continued. "These

evil men target the young, good looking, and the pure, especially Christian children."

"Why?"

"Look at it through a Biblical lens, and it makes sense. The enemy hates God. The purest form of God's children are, well, Christian children."

I wanted to vomit. "We live in a sick horrid world, Drake."

"Yup. Come now Lord Jesus." He exhaled as if he was drained from recalling the sickening statistics. "I'll sniff around from my end. I just hope you got an FBI group assigned to the case who will eat, drink, and sleep this case."

"If you hear of anything let me know?"

"Of course," he said.

"Thanks Drake."

"Talk soon my friend."

My sense of urgency with the case tripled. I texted JT to ask about the guy the FBI had in custody. He texted right back saying the pervert Jeffers still claimed he acted alone. I responded with two words, *no way*. The coincidence was too obvious. JT asked if I had any thoughts, or leads, and I replied with an answer close to a fib and said I was still working on it.

I peered inside Mom's room. She sat up in bed as Dad fed her some yogurt. She was dressed in a hospital issued nightgown with her hair up in a perfect bun.

"You heard the news," she said without looking over.

I was surprised she saw me out of the corner of her eye. "I heard," I said, entering the room.

"I don't want you to worry, Brandon."

"I'm fine."

"I know you," she took another bite of yogurt and

wiped her mouth with a napkin. "You'll internalize this and give yourself an ulcer."

"Only you'd be worried about others during a time like this."

"She's an amazing woman," my dad said holding another spoonful of yogurt to her lips.

"Son," my mother said, "I want you to go home and take care of your pregnant wife."

"I'm not leaving you."

"There's nothing you can do here. The biopsy is in the morning. Why don't you come back then?"

"She's right Brandon," my dad said. "One of us should be on the farm. I'll call you if I hear of anything."

"Do you want me to bring you any clothes or anything?"

"I'm good," my mom said. "When you come back in the morning just bring my hairbrush."

I turned to my dad who said, "I'm fine. I have a shave kit in my truck along with extra clothes."

"I'll have my phone on," I said, "and will be back first thing in the morning. I love you both."

My mother responded likewise, but my dad just nodded. He didn't look at me as his eyes were filling up. For the entire drive back to the farm I was in prayer. I felt like we were under some sort of condemnation from God. First Brooke was abducted and now my mother was in the hospital with a tumor on her kidney. I reminded myself that God didn't work that way with people walking in righteousness, and that this was my sin nature pouring out fear. A passage from First John came to mind reminding me that perfect love drives out fear.

At home I drove directly to the barn and started up a tractor. When I looked up, a shadowy outline of Annie blocked my exit like a pregnant centurion of old. I shut the tractor down.

She walked over and reached for my hand. "Talk to me?"

"I think it's cancer."

She lost her composure for a second before pressing me. "You think, or you know?"

"There's a mass on her kidney. A tumor. They're doing another scan today to confirm and then a biopsy in the morning. If it is cancer they'll do a PET scan to check her entire body to see if it spread."

"Okay, so it could just be a benign tumor, right?"

"I guess."

"Then we need to focus on what we know."

"What I know is she felt pain for a week, and all of a sudden she's nearly immobile. Whatever this is, it's fast-moving, Annie." Try as I might to stop from crying my body ignored the effort. "I just know it's cancer, and it's spreading."

Annie raised my hand to her lips and kissed it. She prayed, "Take therefore no thought for the morrow: for the morrow shall take thought for the things of itself. Sufficient unto the day *is* the evil thereof."

"Amen," I said. I wiped my eyes, kissed my wife, and started up the tractor again.

"Are you sure you need to be doing work right now?" Annie seemed to stop herself before adding, "It's where you relax isn't it?"

I nodded, and the pregnant guard moved aside. Outside, I placed a couple of fence posts in the tractor bucket and headed out to the pastures. For the next few hours I was content to work with my hands. The cows wandered up to the work area, looking for treats. The sky was dark and a drizzle teased me with off and on showers.

After the posts were replaced, I drove the massive main pasture, which was lined with a wire fence. It only needed a few areas tightened.

Back at the barn I put the tractor away and replaced the two grease fittings on the larger tractor. I did a quick workout before closing up the barn for the night. For dinner Annie had made lamb and roast potatoes. She knew it was one of my favorites and was clearly doing everything she could to care for me. I kissed her lips and her belly and tried to joke about John Wayne Hall, but the joke fell flat and no one laughed.

"Is Grammy gonna be okay?" Emily said, washing off her dinner plate.

"I think she's got a rough road ahead of her," I said, "but there's been a lot of advances in medicine." The response I gave didn't seem to satisfy Emily so I added. "I hope so baby."

For dessert, we sat on the porch to eat apple crisp. The drizzle had turned into a light rain which made a rhythmic noise on the tin roof above us. As a farmer and a Christian, the sound of water was mostly associated with good things. Growth, birth, renewal, rejuvenation, and baptism. But there were instances in life, and in the Bible, where water signified judgement and death, such as Noah's flood, and the destruction of Pharaoh's army in the Red Sea. In the distance, the setting sun fought against dark rain clouds to cast a blood-red aura over the property. Within minutes, the light seemed to submit to the darkness.

FIVE

THE NEXT MORNING, I WAS UP AT FIVE A.M. I HAD TOSSED around most of the night thinking about Mom and ended up on the couch around midnight. There were no messages on my cell. I made coffee and tried to eat a granola bar, but only made it halfway through before my appetite left.

In the dim morning light, I could see the cows congregated in one big herd near the small pond. I stepped onto the porch and watched the steam drift upward from the coffee. The air was cool and crisp, free of humidity. I was content in my little farm bubble in the country and did not want to step off the porch into the outside world where death and suffering existed. I knew this was a facade. Death had come to the farm at one point in my recent past, both violence and death. Nowhere on earth was safe from evil.

Coffee in hand, I took a breath and stepped onto the gravel driveway. My 1976 F250 truck Emily nicknamed Hazel had a loud glass-packed muffler, so I depressed the clutch and let her roll down the driveway in neutral. Once on the street I popped the clutch and jump-started the truck with what sounded like gunfire in the quiet country setting.

When I arrived at the hospital, Mom was being prepped in her room. A nurse, a doctor, an orderly, and my dad were all in prayer over my mother who lay in bed with her eyes shut. A large man well over six feet tall led the prayer. Although he was an orderly who had no medical degree it was clear, at that moment, he was in charge.

"Lord, I pray boldly in your son's name for the healing of Mrs. Hall." He reached out a massive hand to touch an Indian doctor's shoulder next to him. "Give doc Patel's hands guidance as he goes in to attack this vestige of sin which is a result of the fall."

Everyone said, *amen.* The giant picked up my mom like she was a piece of paper and laid her gently in the wheelchair.

Mom saw me and reached for my hand. "Did you hear that prayer, Brandon?"

"It was great," I said.

Mom patted the giant on his muscular arm. "Nygel, this is my son I told you about."

"Nice to meet you."

The doctor stepped up to shake my dad's hand. "We'll take care of her, Mr. Hall."

My dad nodded, clearly too upset to say anything. The doctor shook my hand and exited with the nurse.

Before Dad left, he said, "Gonna be a day of prayer, Son."

"Yes, sir."

"I'll walk with your mom as far as they'll let me."

"I'll meet you in the cafe," I said.

For the first time in my life Dad looked small walking behind the orderly pushing Mom. In the cafe I forced myself to eat a bagel. I prayed for God to give Mom good news. Selfishly, I wasn't ready to let her go.

A short while later Dad sat down with a cup of black coffee. He looked like he hadn't slept at all the night before. I hadn't thought about him.

"How are you holding up, old man?" He shrugged his broad shoulders. "That good?"

"I need to think of something other than a scalpel going into your mom right now," he said. "What do you have going on with Brooke Eldridge's case?"

"Not much, I've been distracted with mom-"

My dad held up his hand. "Don't sit back on this one, Son. You gotta jump in the scrum and get dirty. A little girl's life is at stake. A little girl we both know."

I wanted to give him a dozen excuses to justify my lethargy starting with Annie's pregnancy, Emily's home-school, Mom's condition, and the farm, but I realized he was right. I'd been sitting back waiting for a phone call from JT telling me Brooke was safe but heard nothing. I had transcribed my notes to my phone and read what I had. Dad listened like an alert soldier, only moving to take sips of coffee.

"I can't help but think the guy they have in custody is the lynchpin," I said, putting the phone away. "He's gotta know who the other person is who abducted Brooke."

"Why do you say that?"

"What do you mean?" My dad didn't respond. Instead he shrugged his broad shoulders. I pressed him further. "You think it's a coincidence?"

"Maybe."

"No way," I said. "Is it possible? Yes. Is it plausible? Absolutely not. Do you know what the chances of two random independent sickos trying to abduct two children from the same place at the same time are? It's never happened as far as I know. They must know one another."

"Maybe so," Dad said. "The problem is the feds are likely focusing on the guy they have in custody, which is what you're doing."

"So?"

"So, maybe you put on a tin foil hat and start thinking outside the box for a few minutes while they pursue the traditional route?"

"And what? Treat this like it's two completely separate crimes that happened at the same location?"

"Why not? It's a starting point, and you got nothing else."

"You have a point there."

"Your buddy JT owns a self-storage facility on Webster Street, right?" I nodded. "That's only a few blocks from here?"

"Yeah."

"Just keep your cell phone on in case I get an update about your mom." I started to rebuke him, but Dad waved his hand. "We're helpless here. Go do something productive, Son."

Ten minutes later I pulled into Cozy Cavern Self Storage on Webster St. JT was just opening up for the day. He saw my old truck and waved me inside. I placed a cup of coffee down in front of him. He looked like he'd been a prisoner of war. His scruff was turning into a beard and what little hair was on his head was disheveled.

"You're an answer to prayer," he said, taking the coffee with two hands like I had just given him water after a month in the desert.

"Anything new from the feds?" I said.

He shook his head. "Nothing. By the way, Sally's lying

down in the back room, so we need to keep our voices down."

"How's she holding up?"

"I'm really worried about her. She's barely eaten or slept. I'm struggling to keep it together myself." He wiped his eyes with the sleeve of his long sleeve Boston Bruins tee shirt. "I can't stop thinking of Brooke and where she might be right now. I never thought I'd love that girl as much as I do." JT dug in his pocket and tossed a small velvet box on the desk. I knew it was an engagement ring before I opened it. The ring was gorgeous, at least two karats and shined like it had a light embedded in its center. JT started to cry. "I'd already asked Brooke's permission to marry her mom. She was so happy, Brandon. I was gonna take them both out to dinner in Richmond after the home-school convention, and now she's—"

"JT, we gotta stay positive."

"Have you looked at the percentages on the internet?" He opened a laptop on the desk and started to read. "Seventy-five percent of abduction murders occur within three hours after the child goes missing. The majority of non-family abductions are motivated for sexual intentions. And listen to this—"

I shut his laptop. "Stop this."

"What? Educating myself?"

"It's not helping find her right now."

JT rose from behind the desk and looked taller than his five foot seven stature. "Then give me something to hang my hat on."

I blurted out, "What if this guy they have in custody told the truth?"

JT sat back down as if my words had a physical impact. "What do you mean?"

My mind caught up with my statement, and I started to

piece together my dad's idea to come up with a scenario. "What if Jeffers acted alone?"

"With all due respect, your theory defies all probability and is, forgive me, stupid."

I knew JT was upset and didn't take the jab personally. "The FBI is focusing on Jeffers like he knows something. What if he doesn't know anything?"

JT shook his head. "FBI is confident they can break him with some sort of plea deal to spill who his partners were. This is what they do for a living."

"And if they're wrong, it means they start over. It can't hurt just to think about an alternative scenario for a minute. You haven't even heard what I have to say-"

"Come on. You're smarter than this, Brandon."

A soft voice spoke from the back hallway. "Listen to him, JT." We both turned to see Sally standing in the doorway. She had always been a curvy woman but now looked thin. Her face was pale and gaunt. She leaned on the door frame as if it were the only thing holding her up. "Just listen to him," she repeated.

"Here," I said, getting up so Sally could sit in the chair.

"Fine," JT said. "What do you suggest, Brandon?"

"For starters, can you hack into Jeffers' network and poke around his accounts?"

"No chance," JT said. "I'm as good as any NSA weenie, but it would be impossible for me to hack into his stuff at this point."

"Why?"

"FBI have seized all his technology. At this point they've tried, and hopefully succeeded, to hack all his hardware and social media accounts."

"And?"

"And we've been told he was on numerous child porn sites," Sally said.

"Numerous, as in over nine hundred," JT huffed. "Most of which are held on servers in Southeast Asia. FBI can only glean a few pieces of intel off of them. The only chance we have is what the FBI has been saying. We need Jeffers to spill what he knows, and who he knows."

"What are you thinking, Brandon?" Sally said.

"For the time being, why don't we look at this as two separate crimes rather than one."

"Brother, what do you always tell me?"

"That I don't believe in coincidences," I . said, still trying to put my thoughts into a cohesive sentence. "But what if it was a coincidence from one person's point of view."

"Who?" JT said.

"The guy in custody," Sally finished, clearly unable to say Jeffers by name.

I snapped my fingers and pointed to Sally. "Right. What if Jeffers was nudged somehow to hit this convention, but little did he know that he was being set up to act as a distraction?"

"How?"

"Maybe he got into a perv chat room somewhere where they talked about the best places to abduct children and someone randomly threw out homeschool conventions, how they weren't secure, and had no video surveillance when outdoors. Maybe someone knew Jeffers lived in Richmond and knew the convention was upcoming and planted the thought in his head?"

"Why go through so much work to try to manufacture a false flag in Richmond?" JT said.

"Because the other person had a specific reason to hit this specific convention and wanted as many distractions as possible."

"And the reason is?"

"They were targeting Brooke," Sally said, placing her hand over her chest.

"Whoever it was saw Brooke and became obsessed," I said. "Then found out she was going to be at the convention and planned the abduction, but to make sure of a clean getaway they wanted a diversion."

"That's quite a conspiracy theory," JT said.

"It is," I admitted, "but what's the other phrase I always say?"

"Evil doesn't sleep."

Sally raised her hand to her mouth like she was going to vomit. "You mean someone's been stalking my little girl?"

"Only if this scenario is true," I clarified. "If it is, then they must have seen her somewhere, or online." I stepped up to JT's whiteboard and grabbed a marker. "Where do you store your pictures? The cloud?"

"I've checked and it's beyond secure," JT said.

I turned to Sally. "You said you share some pics on social media with private family groups?" Sally nodded. "Do you have anyone close to you that is—" I paused to choose my next word carefully. "Sketchy?"

Sally thought for a moment and nodded a *no*.

A text went off on my phone. Mom was almost out of surgery. Dad offered no more information. I didn't want to burden JT and Sally with my family problems and just said that I had to be somewhere.

My final words to them were, "Keep thinking. There's something we're missing."

SIX

Back at the hospital I found Dad in the small lounge down the hall from Mom's room. He stared out the window at the traffic on route 501. For the first time in my life I thought he looked old. His shoulders were a bit hunched and his hair had more grey than I remembered.

"How's Mom?"

He looked at his watch. "Someone's gonna let me know when I can go into recovery to be there when she wakes up."

"When does the biopsy come back?"

"Takes twenty-four hours but initial thoughts are that it's renal cell carcinoma. They aren't supposed to say anything, but I pressured the doc."

"Cancer," I said, collapsing into a nearby leather chair. Cancer was one of the worst words anyone could hear. "Any plan if-"

"Won't know anything else until they confirm the biopsy and do a PET scan, Son. If it's isolated, then they go in and remove the kidney. If it's metastasized then we're in trouble."

An hour later, Mom was back in her room resting. She floated in and out of sleep. Once, she asked how the biopsy went and Dad said that she did great and that we'd know more the next day. After she fell back asleep Dad quietly prayed over her. He appeared just as frail beside her still form in bed. It was like his life force was tethered to hers.

"I ever tell you how I met your mom," he whispered, kissing her hand.

"It was a military dance, right?"

He nodded. "She was stunning. A debutant that all the men lined up to talk to. I waited in line like all the other guys. She spent the most amount of time talking to me, which I took as a good sign. I figured the other guys were showering her with platitudes, so I took a different approach and made her laugh."

"What did you say?"

He grinned. "I said that I'd understand if she chose one of the other men over me because it was always prudent to go for security rather than good looks." I quietly slapped my knee and stifled a laugh. My dad continued to caress her hand like it was an antique porcelain doll's.

A doctor came in to check my mom's vitals. They cleared their throat and I turned to see Jamie Graham from church.

"I thought you were an OBGYN doc?" I said.

"I saw your mom on the roster this morning and pulled a few strings to come up here," she whispered. "I wish you Halls weren't so private." She finished writing something on a clipboard, fixed my mom's blanket, and motioned for me and my dad to follow her into the hallway. Once outside she said. "Everyone at church is going to know your mom's here."

"How?" My dad said.

"Oh, I'm gonna tell them." The petite twenty-nine-year-old held up a finger barely reaching my dad's chin. "And I'm not apologizing. I won't go into detail due to patient privacy laws unless you guys give me the okay, but everyone needs to know she's here and they'll be waiting for me to tell them what you need." Neither of us responded. "I heard about the preliminary findings on the tumor. Kidney cancer is treatable if they catch it in time, but prepare yourselves. This could be a marathon rather than a sprint. I suggest you take me up on my offer."

My dad looked down at the young spitfire tapping her foot and chuckled. "You're too good to us."

Jamie turned to me, her hand on her hip. "Are you gonna say what you need, or do I need to guess?"

"Okay," I said, holding my arms up in a surrender fashion. "I'm sure Annie could use some help as I have her checking the herd, along with her other responsibilities of homeschooling Emily."

"You have my heavily pregnant patient checking your cattle?"

"Well, she drives a UTV around and takes some notes?"

Jamie pulled out a cell phone. "I'll text Ashley and Tracy who'll get you guys some meals. Brian can swing by your farm after he's done on his dairy farm to check your herd." As Jamie typed away, she said, "How's my patient doing?"

"Annie's doing well," I said. "Still tries to do a small walking loop in the farm each day."

Jamie continued to type on her cell phone. "Great, but make sure she doesn't overdo it." She walked away without saying goodbye.

My dad turned to me. "She's intimidating."

"Thank the Lord we have her and our church."

"Amen."

In a strange way, it was nice to be forced to sit with my dad and mom. It was quality time pulled from a depressing event. Mom ate a light lunch of toast and chicken soup. Every hour or so either Dad or I went for a walk outside for fresh air. Us Halls couldn't survive out of our natural habitat for extended periods of time. We needed to smell hay and grass, breathe fresh air, and see water. I sent Annie a text with an update. She responded right away with prayers the biopsy would contradict the doctor's initial thoughts. Her optimism was comforting.

A nurse came in to wash Mom and I recused myself to the small hallway lounge. I started to review the notes on my cell phone again about Brooke. A part of me kept thinking how vast the FBI's resources were and to trust them. Still, another part of me kept thinking, *what if they're wrong?*

I went home that night and drove the farm before the sun set. A lot needed to be done, but it could wait. The cattle were fine and had more than enough water and grass to fill their bellies. Emily played by the barn with Fescue. It was hard to tell which of them had more energy. Inside, Annie typed on a laptop in the kitchen. She published a monthly farm blog for extra cash. Her focus this month was how to prepare for the arrival of a baby while home-schooling another child.

"How's the article coming, Lois Lane?"

"Slow. I'm trying to recall what I front-loaded in preparation for Jonah's birth."

"Don't forget I'm gonna help with Emily's home-schooling once he's born."

"Most people don't have a husband who works on site. I'm writing this article mostly for moms whose husbands commute to a nine-to-five job somewhere off-property."

My cell phone interrupted the conversation. The call came up as *unknown* which usually meant my friend Agent

Drake was calling from a landline somewhere. I put it on speakerphone. "Brandon Hall speaking?"

"Mr. Hall, it's your stylishly suave friend from D.C. calling."

I walked out onto the porch to give Annie some privacy. "What's up?"

"Are you alone?"

I took it off speakerphone. "I am now."

"Your friend from South Boston whose daughter is missing. Her full name is Sally Eldridge correct?"

"Yeah, why?"

"This is a long shot but bear with me. A lot of child abductions involve sex trafficking, which got me thinking."

My stomach tightened just hearing those two words. "I know."

"The sex trafficking industry has deep ties to the abortion industry. You get these young girls who get drugged up and pregnant and the handlers need to dispose of the baby while keeping it on the down low."

"That's sick."

"Sad to say it's very true." He continued, "So the sex trafficking abortion connection got me thinking. I did a search on Sally Eldridge's family tree and cross-referenced it with a nationwide database of people who've had abortions and-"

"Wait a second," I cut in. "You're telling me the government can access that information?"

There was a pause on the other end of the phone. "Brandon, you'd die if you knew how much intel Big Brother had access to. Put it this way, there are very few things the government doesn't know about you."

"That's just wrong," I said.

"Hundred percent agree, but it's the world we live in right now. So, do you want to hear my theory?"

"I'm sorry. Of course."

"I found two names that were relatives of Sally who've had abortions, and both are east coast. I'll send you their names when we get off the phone."

"How do you think this could tie in with Brooke's disappearance?"

"This is just my personal theory."

"Shoot."

"A lot of child abductions are by people with ties to the family."

"The FBI has looked into this-"

"Don't be so sure. I think they'll go to immediate kin and some other red-flag relatives but then focus back on the guy they have in custody. What I'm suggesting is a few more degrees of separation. Hidden red flags they won't be looking for due to our politically correct culture."

"Okay."

"It's a fact that abortion rates are higher with girls who come from divorced homes, but this is where much of the secular research ends. However, new research is starting to collect data on abortion rates tied to dysfunctional homes where one, or both, parents are dealing with things like alcohol or drug abuse."

"Makes sense."

"Stay with me," Drake said. "I believe there's another tier to this. Where percentages are even greater from homes with high dysfunction."

"High dysfunction?"

"Homes with people dealing in sex abuse, and even child porn. It's a long shot but sit with Miss Eldridge and ask about these two cousins. If either of them came from this type of home, there could be something deeper there with their friends and associates."

"Can you send this info along to the FBI?"

"In my, uhm, unique position I can float in and out of most government agencies, but this division of the FBI is locked tight. Besides, I'd rather you look into it first as it's a long shot."

"Are you ever going to tell me what department you work for?"

He laughed on the other end of the phone but didn't answer the question. "I'll let you know if I think of anything else, otherwise I'll be in prayer for Sally and Brooke. By the way, how's your momma?"

"Docs did a biopsy and initial thought is cancer. Will know more in next twenty-four hours."

"I know top docs up and down the east coast if we need them. Keep me posted."

"Thank you."

After hanging up I realized Drake used the pronoun *we* before he hung up. The man wasn't afraid to get dirty and help out. I was beyond blessed to have someone like him in my life. The country would be in a far better place if the government could recruit more people like Drake. A moment later the two names scrolled across my phone. One had the last name Eldridge, the other's last name was Swanson. Both were women in their mid-twenties. One had an abortion in her late teens and the other was at fourteen. How I'd broach this topic with Sally would be odd, and like Drake said, it was a long shot.

I took a shower as if to wash the filth of the conversation out of my mind. I hated everything about this case. I hated knowing the family, and hated that I had to learn about human trafficking as part of my research. I wanted to retreat into my simple life on the farm. When I finally crawled into bed, I made the mistake of checking my phone one more time. There was a text from Dad with two words.

Cancer confirmed.

After a restless night's sleep, I awoke at seven-thirty which was late for a farmer. Annie was on the porch with a bowl of oatmeal and a cup of tea reading her devotional with a cashmere shawl draped over her bathrobe. Her dark hair was in a ponytail and she wore no makeup, but she had a glow that radiated a healthy pregnancy. Fescue ran on a line back and forth from the porch to a large oak tree.

"I ever tell you how beautiful you look in the morning," I said, taking up a seat next to her with a cup of coffee.

Annie finished reading and closed her Bible before she turned to me. "Thanks, sweetie."

I kissed her head, then her belly. I stayed on my knees to talk to my child. "Your momma's got her pregnancy glow going on little man."

"What do you think of the name Lara?"

"Great name if we get another dog," I said, "but I think he's a John Wayne Hall."

"Addison?"

"Not bad."

"Wow," Annie said, grabbing her stomach. "He just moved?"

"Ha," I said, placing my hand on her belly. "You said he." There was more movement then nothing. "Think he's okay?"

"He's fine," she said. "How is it you're in a panic and I'm the calm one?"

"I think we're swapping personalities," I said, getting up. "I'm heading to the hospital."

"Any news on your mom?"

"I didn't want to bother you last night, but Dad texted me before bed confirming it was cancer."

"Oh, dear Lord," Annie said.

"Before you ask, you and Emily are not coming with

me. Your immune system is lower being pregnant and the last place I want you is where sick people congregate. I'll keep you guys updated via texts."

"What's the plan?"

"I think they're doing a PET scan today to see if it's anywhere else. If the cancer is isolated at stage one, then they remove the kidney and maybe hit it with radiation. Stage two and beyond means it's spread and then it's a crap shoot which may involve multiple docs, multiple surgeries, and a variety of treatments, one of which will probably be chemotherapy."

"Then my prayers are clear for the day."

Emily came outside yawning. She and Fescue locked eyes and ran to one other. "Did you miss Momma last night baby girl?" The puppy went into overdrive and jumped all over Emily. "Okay, let's get you some breakfast." Emily walked past us holding the squirming puppy like it was a newborn.

"Another Hall woman and her baby," I said, turning to Annie. "You still upset I got her the puppy?"

"It's hard when the dog is that cute."

I made Emily and me oatmeal and the three of us sat on the porch as the chill of dawn morphed into a warm morning.

"Daddy, can I come to the hospital with you?"

"I don't think it's—"

"I'll bring my homeschool work and stay out of the way. I'll say hi to Grammy and won't bug her."

"Might be good for your mom to see her," Annie added.

"Ok," I said, "but if you get bored, I'm not driving you home."

"That's fine."

"No complaining," I added.

"I promise."

"Okay, get your things."

Emily ran off inside like I had just told her we were going to Kings Dominion Amusement Park up in Richmond. "Ahh, childhood enthusiasm," I said.

"Gotta love it," Annie added.

Emily and I drove over to my parents' log cabin to pick up some spare clothes. I checked the small paddock out back to make sure my dad's horse had oats and water while Emily checked the small chicken coop to collect eggs and check the gravity fed food and water feeders.

Inside the cabin was a small two-bedroom single-story structure my dad built so he and my mom could downsize. They had the spare bedroom furnished with bunk beds and a single twin bed for the multiple grandchildren they expected me, and Annie, to produce. Every wall and counter was covered with pictures of Emily, Annie, and me at various stages of my life. There were only a couple of pictures of my dad and mom modestly placed behind the others. One of which sat on the mantel over my dad's flint-lock rifle. It was a black and white photo that looked like a vintage picture from the forties. Gary Cooper and Grace Kelly had nothing on my parents. My dad wore his military whites and my mom was in a stunning wedding dress accented modestly with lace. They looked so handsome together. I wasn't ready to let either of them go.

"Daddy, look at this," Emily said, holding a small framed picture of my infant son, Jonah.

Jonah was in a diaper and had just dumped out a box of cereal all over the floor. He had a smirk on his chubby face as if to say, *how can you be mad at me?* On the same shelf were more pictures of him. My mom was careful not to have them front and center so as to not upset Annie. A drunk driver on route 501 ended my son's life. Annie only suffered superficial physical wounds, but the mental wounds were far worse. I thought she would never come back from the abyss she fell into after we lost him. I wiped the dust off the picture and placed it back on the shelf in the front.

"I miss him," Emily said.

If I responded, I knew it would come out with tears. Instead, I picked up the bag of clothes and motioned for her to follow me back out to the truck.

SEVEN

At the hospital, Mom's face lit up when she saw Emily. She kept kissing her and saying how much she loved her. Emily snuggled up against Mom in her bed like a kitten.

"I prayed for a healthy grandchild," Mom said, "but God blessed me with a healthy child who happens to be the most beautiful girl in the world."

"She definitely takes after her mom," Dad said.

Everyone laughed.

Someone cleared their throat behind us. We all turned to see Jamie standing with an orderly. "I got permission to walk you to the PET scan."

Mom smiled and seemed at peace. I was in awe of her strength and faith. Within twenty-four hours of the scan Mom would be told if the cancer was contained or had spread. Theoretically, the news would be one of three results. The first was if the cancer was contained and she would live. The second scenario was if it had spread a little. Here she would possibly live, but a percentage would be attached to it. The final scenario was if the cancer had spread throughout her body. This would more than likely have a timeframe, rather than a percentage, attached to it. I kissed Mom and left the room with Emily. We went to the cafe and spread her homework out on a table. I got a cup of coffee and an orange juice for Emily.

As Emily went through her math homework, I borrowed a piece of paper and a pencil to write down some of my cell phone notes on Brooke's case. How would I present the two people Drake sent over to Sally? *Hey Sally, I know your daughter's missing and you haven't slept in days but let's talk about your two cousins who've had abortions.*

My father came into the cafe and got a cup of black coffee. "Mom's getting the scan now," he said, sitting down next to Emily. "What are you working on, sweetie?"

"Stupid math." Emily exhaled in a sarcastic tone only she could pull off.

"It isn't stupid." My dad looked at her book. "You just don't understand how you'll need it."

"When am I ever going to use this stuff in life?"

"If you want to be a farmer then you'll use it every day," I said.

"Otherwise you'll go out of business," my dad added. "You have to be able to calculate crops, animals, projected income, expenses and be able to follow the markets. There's not a day that goes by that I don't use math." He pointed to a word problem in her book. "This is asking you about raffle tickets and percentages of winning. This has no bearing on Emily Hall, right?"

"Right. It's dumb."

"Don't say dumb," I said.

"Your dad's right," he added. "Now if I were to change the premise of the word problem from raffle tickets to total number of cattle, and changed tickets sold to healthy births. You can now predict how big the herd will grow next year. Once you do this, you can then forecast income and expenses. You'll also need to predict a percentage for COLA."

"COLA?"

"Cost Of Living Adjustment," I said. "How much taxes will go up, feed, fuel, etc."

Emily put her pencil down. "I never thought of it like that."

"Your grandfather used to teach this stuff when he was in the military," I said. "He's much smarter than he looks." My dad smiled and Emily laughed. "Dad, can you hang with Emily for a bit while I shoot down the street to see my buddy?"

"Of course," he said. "I'd appreciate the company."

"Can I go?" Emily said.

"No honey, this is work stuff and you need to finish your schoolwork."

"Keep your old grandad company," Dad added.

I closed the deal by promising Emily a donut from the bakery across the street from the hospital. Ten minutes later I found JT in his office on Webster Street. Sally was there again. Both of them looked like they had been on drunken benders the night before. I knew it was a combination of stress and lack of sleep.

"What's the latest from the FBI?" I said, hoping they had something.

"Nothing. You got anything, brotha?"

"What I have is a long shot, so bear with me for what I'm about to ask. It's personal."

"Brandon, I don't care," Sally said. "Ask me anything."

I read the two names off of the piece of paper. "Tell me about Erin Eldridge and Sue Swanson?"

"My cousins?" Sally said, clearly confused. "What would they have to do with this?"

I winced knowing what I had to say next was very

personal and felt gossipy. "Both of them had abortions. Erin in her late teens and Sue in her early twenties."

"I never knew," Sally said.

JT perked up. "What's the correlation here, brotha?"

"Like I said it's a long shot, but many times girls who have abortions come from broken homes. Are either of their families divorced?"

"Both of their parents are, why?"

I could see JT's posture straighten as if he were connecting mental dots. A moment later he blurted out, "Brandon thinks maybe one of the dads are into child pedo stuff."

I winced at JT's gruff explanation and tried to re-state it. "A lot of child abductions are from people close to the families. You said the only people you share social media pics of Brooke with are some closed family groups, right?"

"Yeah."

"Are these two cousins on either of them?"

"Erin is?"

"Do you think she could share those pics with others in her family?"

"I guess it's possible."

"What can you tell me about her father?"

"Nothing really. He's related to me by marriage, and Erin's not close with him. He got divorced from Erin's mom a while back."

JT cut in, "Any pedo stuff going on?"

"I don't think so. Then again, he was a scumbag who cheated on Erin's mom all the time. Got remarried to one of the ladies he cheated on her with."

"Maybe we should talk to your cousin, Erin?" I said.

"She moved down to Tarpon Springs, Florida."

"Forget her," JT said, starting to get up. "We don't have the time. Where's her dad living?"

Sally motioned for JT to sit down. "He can't be involved."

"Why?"

"I heard that he died about a month ago from a heart attack." I sunk back in my seat. The long shot had now become an impossible shot. "He lived in Halifax with his current wife if you want to go talk to her."

"Guys, this was thin to begin with," I said, "and it just became a near impossible-"

"We got nothing better to do," JT said.

Sally added. "You're not leaving me here alone."

"I'll drive," JT said, looking at me for approval.

I knew Sally and JT needed something to occupy their minds. This scenario was no longer tenable, but if it helped keep their sanity then I'd go down this rabbit hole. My hope was that while we pursued the dead-end the FBI got closer to finding Brooke.

"Okay," I said. "Let's go talk to this woman."

The three of us piled into JT's SUV. It was a brand new vehicle with shiny black leather seats. Easily a sixty-thousand-dollar ride. My friend had made a fortune up north in the tech world and purchased the self-storage facility to keep his sanity after his wife left him. For a full year after moving to South Boston he didn't touch a computer, or cell phone. Eventually, he started dabbling in the programming world again.

It only took a few minutes to make it into downtown Halifax. We passed by the small local shops in hundred-year-old brick buildings and turned onto LP Bailey Memorial Highway. A few miles after crossing the bridge over Bannister Lake we found the address. The home was a small white ranch in need of repairs. There was an old pickup in the driveway that looked to be from the 1980s.

JT parked and we both hung back while Sally approached the front door.

She knocked on the door before turning to us. "I've never met this woman before."

An older woman answered the door. She was in a bathrobe and had a cigarette dangling from her mouth. She looked like she could be anywhere from fifty to seventy. It was hard to tell, but it was clear the woman had lived a rough life.

She stood behind a screen door with a large hole in it. "Yeah?"

"Are you Wanda Eldridge?" Sally said. The woman didn't respond. "My uncle was Darren?"

The woman looked over at JT's new SUV with the Cozy Cavern Self Storage lettering then huffed. "I sold all his HAM radio gear and plan on doing the same with his guns and fishing gear, so if you're looking to rummage through the rest of his toys you can forget about it. That jerk riddled me with debt and-"

"No ma'am," I interrupted. "We'd like to have a conversation about something else. Do you mind if we come in?"

"Please," Sally added.

She ran her hand through a mess of hair as if to groom herself. "Fine, but the place is a wreck."

We stepped inside what appeared to be a time warp. The couches and appliances were a strange yellow from either the late 1960s or early 1970s. Boxes were strewn everywhere. Small bits of paper and candy wrappers peeked out from under a couch. The place reeked of smoke and filth. Three cats ate from one big bowl in the small kitchen. Sally and JT sat down with JT holding her hand. I chose to stand; the thought of bed bugs and lice came to mind when I looked at the furniture.

"Do you mind if I ask you some questions about Darren?" Sally said.

"Why?" Wanda almost shouted. "What did that jerk do now?"

I wanted to interrupt, but I could see some life coming back into Sally's eyes.

"I don't know if you've seen my face on the news?" Sally continued. Wanda nodded. "Never seen you before."

"My eight-year-old daughter Brooke was abducted up in Richmond this past week?"

Wanda crushed a half-smoked cigarette into a nearby ashtray and relit another. "I'm sorry for your loss, but what does this have to do with me?"

I spoke up. "Was Darren walking in circles with anyone of ill repute?"

Wanda turned to me and squinted as if I spoke another language. "I'm a simple gal, mister."

"Was he into porn, snuff films, pedo porn or anything like that?" JT said.

I loved JT's directness, but it sometimes came across as rude.

Wanda got up and started towards the front door. "I think you need to leave."

"Please," Sally said, following the woman.

Wanda reached her front door. I expected her to hold it open pointing us to leave but instead she walked out into the front yard. Sally followed her like a puppy. I followed Sally.

"Wanda, if you know something you need to tell me?" Sally said.

Wanda turned on her heel using the cigarette like a pointer. "I don't need to do anything, missy. You have no idea what that man put me through? I lost my job and all my savings from all his crap."

Sally started to cry. "My daughter is missing."

"It has nothing to do with me," Wanda said. "You said her abduction happened in the past week?" Sally nodded. "Well, Darren's been in the ground for a month, so I don't see how he had anything to do with it."

I came up and placed my hand on Sally's shoulder to try to calm her down. "Please, Wanda. We're begging. If you know anything-"

"I know nothing," she said, kneeling down to pick up trash from a garbage can that had fallen over. "You should leave, or else I'm gonna call the police."

I threw up a last-ditch effort and tried the tough guy approach. "We'll come back with the sheriff," I said.

"Try it," she shouted, flicking her cigarette at my chest. It bounced off and fell to the ground. She got up in my face and wagged a bony finger an inch from my jaw. "You just try it and see what happens, you hear? Now get off my property."

"Come on Sally," I said, encouraging her to walk with me back around the house.

JT was in the SUV with the engine running. I helped Sally into the passenger seat before getting into the back seat. JT tore out of the driveway spraying dirt back at the woman who now gave us the finger.

"That went well," JT said.

"She knows something," Sally said.

"Or she's just scared," I said. "She said Darren riddled her with debt. For all we know bookies might be sending strong-arm guys here to shake her down."

"Either way, we'll know by tonight what she knows," JT said. "I got the husband's laptop."

"You did what?" Sally said.

"While you three were arguing outside I wandered into her bedroom, found a storage box with wires hanging out of it, popped the top and grabbed the only laptop in there. I'm assuming it's the husband's."

Sally looked both shocked and impressed. "How'd you think to do that-"

"Misspent youth on the streets of Dorchester."

"But it's stealing?" Sally said. "I don't think it's the Christian thing to do."

"Time ain't our friend, sweetie. God sometimes needs a nudge."

"But-"

"Don't worry. I promise I'll return it."

"Where is it?"

"Brandon's sitting next to it."

Sure enough, next to me was a Boston Red Sox windbreaker and under it was a new laptop. I was impressed with JT's skill, but didn't feel right with the idea of lifting the property.

"If he was into pedo stuff he'd probably be on the dark web. Only way I can get in is if I have his laptop."

"Dark web?" I said.

"It's the part of the Internet that's hidden from search engines. Uses masked IP addresses and it is accessible with only a special browser, which I'm hoping is still on his laptop. It was originally used for military and journalists but quickly devolved into a cesspool of illicit blackmarket industries."

Back at the office JT worked frantically to break into the laptop. "I'm impressed," he said, typing at a furious speed. "The guy has some solid protection in place. I'd go get some coffee if I were you two. This could be a while."

"My daughter's at the Halifax Hospital," I said. "I gotta go pick her up."

JT stopped and looked at me. "She's where? What happened?"

"And why didn't you tell us?" Sally added.

"It's not what you think. My mom had a biopsy and they found a tumor on her left kidney. They're doing a PET scan today and Emily is with her."

Sally started to cry. "I'm so sorry. I feel horrible that you're here and-"

"Don't worry about it. My dad is there with her. I just want to pick Emily up." I grabbed a pad of paper from JT's desk and started writing down instructions. "JT, if you get into the computer-"

"Not a matter of if."

"Then when you get into the computer," I said, "you have to see if he has any pictures of Brooke."

"I can run a program for facial recognition."

I turned to Sally. "Maybe your cousin Erin shared photos with him. That would be our starting point." I turned back to JT. "Then you unfortunately need to look to see if there's porn photos or mp4's and search for websites he may have visited and shared stuff with. If the laptop's clean, then we return the computer."

"And we start over," Sally said, sitting down.

"Once I'm in," JT said, "I can upload everything to the cloud and return the laptop tonight if you'd like."

"I'm still confused how this all ties together if Darren is dead?" Sally said.

"Darren's clearly not the culprit," I said. "But if he had pics of Brooke on his laptop then he may have shared them in a network."

"Pedos are like their own guild and love to share stuff online," JT added. Before anyone could ask how he knew this information he raised a hand as if to say he was inno-cent. "I ran a hi-tech company and had to know about this stuff. You'd be shocked how many of my employees ended up having porn of some kind on their work computers.

Brandon's right though. If we can find pics of Brooke and then a network the pic was shared on, it may allow us access to a pool of IP addresses."

I clarified. "Remember, it's still a long shot."

"But I still don't understand," Sally said. "It's not like I shared any pics of Brooke naked or—"

"What about pics of her up at Buggs Island or Hyco Lake or at a local pool?" I said.

"Pics of her in a bathing suit," JT added. "Anything could trigger a perv to share a pic."

"I feel like I'm going to throw up," Sally said before leaving the room. Thirty-seconds later I realized she wasn't exaggerating when I heard her wretch in the breakout room sink.

I rested my hand on JT's shoulder. He reached up and held fast to my grip for a moment. The stakes were so high. I left without saying a word. Driving back to the hospital, I kept wishing I never knew Sally, Brooke, or JT. This shameful self-preservation sin nature longed to live in a simple world where disease, sickness, and misery didn't exist. Where everyone was healthy and happy. An unrealistic world without the human condition. I knew God promised a day when there would be no more tears or pain or sorrow, but for now I lived in a fallen world that was plagued by evil.

EIGHT

I stopped at a bakery across from the hospital. Inside, the smell was a mixture of flour, sugar, butter and a soft scent that reminded me of wedding cake. It was a deadly combination. I planned on getting Emily a single donut but decided on a half dozen donuts so everyone could have one. Back at the hospital, Mom was in a wheelchair while Dad gathered her belongings. I handed the bag of donuts to Emily. She took out a glazed one and handed the bag to my dad who took out a chocolate one.

"Where you going?" I said, taking a bite of my third donut.

"Home," Mom said.

"Doc will have PET scan results for us in a day or two," Dad said. "Insurance said mom could stay here until surgery, but she demanded to be brought home."

"I'm able to shuffle around with the cane and the pain killers they gave me."

"Then what's the plan?" I said.

"Unless they find something really bad, they are moving forward with the surgery on Monday.

"What do you mean, really bad?"

"If it's spread throughout my body then they may delay surgery," Mom said matter-of-factly. "Or cancel it altogether if it's pervasive."

"You're not going anywhere," I said.

She reached out for my hand. "We're all going somewhere, sweetie."

The woman was strong. Stronger than I'd ever be. It was an amazing contrast to witness this level of strength come from a five foot three inch, hundred-pound woman. I kissed her on the head.

"Can I drive home with Grammy?" Emily said.

"Sure."

My cell text pinged. It was JT saying he got into the computer and uploaded everything to the cloud. He asked if I could grab the laptop to return it after I left the hospital. I texted back stating I would stop by in a few minutes. An orderly wheeled my mom to the front entrance while my dad drove his truck up to meet us. I helped load Mom into the passenger seat. She winced but never complained. Emily jumped into the back seat.

"Be a blessing," I said to Emily.

"Are you coming home?" she said.

"Soon, but I gotta make a stop first."

Back at Cozy Cavern, JT walked the laptop out to me. There was a part of me that was glad I didn't have to go back inside and face Sally. She reminded me too much of Annie after our son was killed.

I took the laptop from JT. "I'll drop this off and apologize to Wanda."

"Thanks, brotha. Everything from the laptop is in the cloud now, but it may take me a while to sift through it all."

"Keep your expectations low," I said. "For all we know

he could have some fishing and hunting journals and nothing else."

"Sally's about to lose it and the FBI communication line is lessening by the hour," JT said. "It's like I'm watching in real-time as Brooke's case is being de-prioritized as new crimes pull on their resources.

"Anything else I can do?" I said.

"Pray, brotha. Pray like never before."

A familiar looking old truck pulled up blocking us in. My hand instinctively dropped under my shirt to my appendix holster. It was the same truck I saw at Wanda's property. I placed the laptop on the passenger seat of my truck. Wanda stepped out still dressed in her bathrobe. A new cigarette hung from her mouth. I was half-expecting police to pull in behind her with lights flashing asking about the stolen computer.

"Mrs. Eldridge, I was just coming back to see you to apologize-"

"That son of perdition put me through hell," she said, cutting me off. "I lost everything because of him."

"What do you mean?" I said.

"I had nothing to do with no children," was the only answer she gave. She reached into the cab of the truck and pulled out a cardboard box with wires hanging out of it. She handed it to JT. "Here's all his electronics. If you find anything, I don't want to know about it." She flicked the cigarette into a nearby rose bush and was about to say something, but instead got into her truck and tore out.

I placed the laptop back into the box and handed it to JT. "So God needs a nudge, does he?"

"I'm being proven wrong on a daily basis, dude." He started back towards the office. "Can you hang for a bit while I search through what I just downloaded?"

"Sure. I was just gonna go get us a couple of coffees."

"That would be a Godsend."

Ten minutes later I entered Cozy Cavern's office door carrying three coffees. JT held a finger to his lips to tell me to be quiet. "Sally's resting in the back room." He motioned for me to pull the chair around his desk where he worked on his laptop.

"What did you find?"

"I found tons of porn."

I winced. "Child porn?"

He nodded. "Sick stuff brotha. I'm running a program that will do facial recognition and let me know if it picks up Brooke's face."

JT's laptop looked like a cross between a steam punk typewriter and something from Star Trek. The hourglass image on the center of the large screen kept showing that it was searching hundreds of files per second. The entire time I prayed we would find some clue. Suddenly, it stopped. A single picture of Brooke popped up. She was in a tankini and appeared to be at a swimming pool at a local park. It wasn't anything risqué, and had an innocent caption accompanying it which Sally wrote, "They grow up so quick".

"Bingo," JT said, typing on the laptop. "Doesn't appear there are any other pictures of Brooke."

"Now what?"

"Now let's see if the pic was shared anywhere."

JT typed at a furious speed. Applications and programs opened and closed in flashes. I had no idea what the code popping up on the screen meant. Watching my short chubby friend work in this environment was like watching Tom Brady play football. JT's typing increased, and by the force with which he hit the keys, it was apparent he was frustrated.

"Guy has been on a ton of websites that are all over the place."

"This pic of Brooke still doesn't mean anything," I said.

"My gut tells me otherwise, brotha." JT stopped typing for a moment and turned to me. "Weren't you the same dude busting my chops about the need to be optimistic?"

"Sorry. I don't know what my problem is."

"I need you all-in," he said, turning back to the screen. "Sally needs you." He stopped typing and looked at me again. "Brooke needs you."

"I'm sorry. I never enjoy investigating this side of humanity."

"You're full of crap."

"I'm sorry," I said, realizing I couldn't lie to my friend. "For some reason this just keeps dredging up memories of my son. I'm sorry, JT. I feel so weak."

"You're not weak, you're human." JT said. "I know this is difficult for you, but I'll get on my knees and beg if you need me to-"

I rested my hand on his shoulder. "I'm with you to the end."

JT went back to work; his soft rebuke having worked. A minute later he said, "Bingo."

"What?"

"Our Mr. Eldridge has been on hundreds of websites, but he's only shared that picture of Brooke with three."

"Why?"

"Probably because Brooke was fully clothed. These demons like nudity."

"Can you access the websites?"

JT typed some more. "I can only get onto the websites if he's cached his passwords. Otherwise they're fortified like Fort Knox."

Within moments JT clapped his hands and pointed to the screen. "I'm in." He scrolled through the first website for a few minutes before logging off. "Brooke's pic was shared but no one commented. I'm going to the second website."

I had to turn away at some of the pictures that Darren Eldridge had saved on this site. They were beyond disturbing. These pictures were rock solid proof in my book that evil was real, it was visceral, and no longer was satisfied with lurking in the shadows. I finally turned back around to face the screen.

"Brooke's pic got some feedback on this site."

"What are you doing now?"

"Trying to hack Darren's messaging capabilities on the site. Here, see. Someone named Beelzebub contacted him about the picture of Brooke."

"Uhm, that name's a bit of a biblical red flag."

"Ya think?" JT said. "So, at one point, Beelzebub asked Darren Eldridge, who goes by Ghost1, if he had any more pics of that cute blond in the bathing suit." JT started to choke up, "He wanted to know if there were any nudes and offered him several pics in exchange."

"I feel like I'm going to vomit," I said. "What did Eldridge reply?"

"He replied no, and that the pic was of a relative and would send more if he could get them." JT typed some more. "Beelzebub replied back with three messages. The first reads, *She's beautiful.* Then he said, *I'm obsessed.* And the third message read, *Let's chat offline.* The conversation ended after that." JT logged on a third website. "This is the last site Darren shared the pic on and doesn't appear to have any feedback or messaging about that pic. Again, probably because she had clothes on."

"Can we go back to the other site and hack into Beelzebub's account to find out where he's out of?"

"Negative," JT said. "The hosting site is too fortified."

"What did he mean by chat offline?"

"Who knows," JT said. "Could be a secure phone line or another secure messaging site. I'm not an expert with this pedo stuff, but I'll poke around some more."

"Keep trying," I said. "If you can get an IP address, I can go to my contact in DC to see if he can turn over some stones."

"Roger that."

On the way home I called Drake. He picked up on the first ring. "Agent Drake, I need a favor."

"What else is new?"

I laughed as he was right. It truly was a one-sided friendship. "That intel you gave me kind of panned out. Long story short, we found one site that a pic of Brooke had been shared on and there were messages between two people. I have a name I may need to be hacked. My tech buddy is working on getting the IP address. Still a long shot but my gut is telling me this is a solid lead."

"Text me the info when you get it and I can pull in favors from a few government nerds I know."

"All I know so far is the guy's name is Beelzebub."

"You're joking."

"Fitting isn't it. I'll text you the name of the website. Talk soon."

A short while later I picked up Emily at my parent's cabin. Dad was on the porch whittling wood with her. Emily was a natural woodsman who loved camping, fishing and anything to do with the outdoors.

"What are you making?" I said, stepping from the truck.

"A fishing pole for the baby," she said.

"You gave Emily your pocketknife?" My dad asked.

"She's old enough," I said, taking out my new knife and

handing it to him. "I think it's time I moved from a gentleman's slip joint to something more substantial."

My dad looked over the knife and nodded his approval before handing it back. I picked up a stick off the porch and started whittling as well. "Where's Mom?"

"Resting inside."

"How's she doing?"

"She's an amazing woman, your mother. Tough as nails. Doesn't seem to be afraid at all. I'd gladly be in a foxhole with that woman any day."

"What do you call her when she yells at you?" Emily said. "The old battle axe?"

My dad blushed. "Let's forget I say that, sweetie."

Annie texted asking for some largemouth bass for dinner. She was making her famous fish tacos.

"Emily, want to help me catch some fish for dinner?"

"Absolutely." She turned to my dad. "Please come, Grampy?"

"I can't sweetie. I gotta stay here to watch over your grandma. Have fun though."

The two of us drove the property to check on the herd and ended up at our main pond. It was a one-acre pond with inflow and outflow and was the only water source on the farm I had fenced off. By keeping the cows out, it kept the water and fish clean. Hundreds of cows dropping dung in your pond makes for dirty water and fish that were not edible. In the truck toolbox I kept a couple of collapsible fishing poles. It was far enough along in spring that crappie and bass were biting. I used a spinner lure while Emily dug up some worms. It only took an hour to catch enough fish for dinner.

Back home we ate dinner out on the porch. The fire pit near the porch fought back the nighttime chill.

"Did you guys have fun fishing?" Annie said.

"It was awesome," Emily said. Turning to me she added. "Daddy, are we still going fishing with Mr. Drake?"

"I forgot to tell you that I had to cancel."

She paused before saying, "Because of Brooke?"

"Yeah."

"Why don't you and Emily just go someplace closer?" Annie said. "You could both use the break."

"I don't feel comfortable with Mom-"

"How about if your mom's surgery goes well then you give yourself a break?"

With no other excuses to think of I nodded agreement. Emily jumped up and down hugging me. "Can we go to Smith Mountain Lake?"

"Sure."

Last summer I had taken Emily up to the lake at the end of summer to introduce her to scuba diving. Along with my private investigating work I did some dive recovery work on the side, a remnant skill I picked up from my time in the Marines. Emily took to anything with the water whether it was fishing, swimming, or even scuba. If she didn't take up farming, I could see her moving closer to the sea. Maybe to the outer banks or Myrtle Beach. I could always tell when someone had saltwater in their veins, and Emily was half mermaid.

After dinner we watched an episode of Little House on the Prairie, a long-time favorite television show of Emily's. In this episode, young Laura Ingalls ran away from home. She tried to climb a mountain to be closer to God so He might hear her prayers better. Along the way she met an old man named Jonathan who happened to be Laura's guardian angel. Jonathan watched over her until Pa found her. The entire episode I kept thinking of Brooke and praying she was still alive and that God had placed her guardian angel close by to watch over her.

Before bed JT texted. It read, 'Could not get an IP address for Beelzebub. Please ask if your government friend can look into the site.' I told JT I would send it along. I texted the name Beelzebub along with the website along to Drake, asking if he could pull some strings to look into it. I said another prayer for Brooke and Sally before another restless night's sleep.

The next morning Dad drove the property with my mom in the passenger seat of his truck. They stayed on the smooth dirt road avoiding the bumpy pastures. I blew Mom a kiss from the back of the tractor as they passed by. She loved the farm, and the fresh air and scenic views would cheer her up. Late morning, I received a text from Drake to call him. My heart raced as I dialed his number.

"What do you have?" I said the moment he picked up.

"Well, good morning to you too, my brother."

"Sorry, I'm just on edge."

"Understandable," Drake said. "I have good news and bad news."

"Always the bad first."

"You didn't give me a whole lot to go on, but I pulled in some serious favors to get to the bottom of this. The website is based in Thailand and is impossible to hack into."

"And?"

"And we couldn't get the IP addresses.

"That is bad news."

"So, I had him do a reverse search of sorts and track any IP addresses from the US that went into that overseas website. Unfortunately, there were tens of thousands."

"And the good news?" I said.

"I had him narrow it down to see if, by chance, any one of the IP addresses was done over a mobile device. This took it from the thousands down to the hundreds. My guy can hack mobile devices no problem. I then had him do a word search for the name Beelzebub. There was only one device that had that word show up on it. We geo-located his device to the Dismal Swamp in southeast Virginia."

"Do you have a location?"

"I'll text it when I get off the phone, and before you ask me, I looked him up. The guy is single, has no family, and no criminal record. Heck, he's barely on the grid. Pays for everything with cash, including his taxes. His name's Jeb Lawson. Forty-year-old, Caucasian male. One brother, Joss, who lives in Elizabeth City, North Carolina. Same profile for Joss. I'm sending over Jeb's address."

"I appreciate it."

"You do realize this entire theory hinges on one dead guy who received an inquiry about a picture?"

"I know."

"And this cell phone we tracked simply had the word Beelzebub show up on it. There's a good chance this Lawson's not the same guy. The chances of anything coming from this are-"

"Slim, I know," I said, "but the girl's mother is barely holding it together. I need to do something."

"Understood. Talk soon."

A minute after Drake hung up, an address in Southfork, Virginia showed up via text. It was at least a two-and-half-hour drive. I had only been to the Dismal Swamp once as a child. The Great Dismal Swamp was named by surveyors back in the 1700s after their horrible experience tracking through it. The most famous surveyor was a young man named George Washington. A bright spot in the swamp's history was when it became a haven for runaway slaves who were called maroons. The environment was so tough for outsiders to penetrate that the former slaves found a little bit of freedom there, and even set up small settlements.

I could only imagine what this guy's property looked like. Images of the Florida Everglades came to mind. Pictures of snakes, stagnant water, and thousands of mosquitos. I could understand why people lived in the mountains, near lakes, by the ocean, heck even in the city, but for the life of me I had no idea why someone would live near a swamp.

The rest of the day was filled with farm chores which were a welcoming distraction. Dinner that night was free-range organic chicken, or as I liked to say, one of my mom's unfortunate hens who stopped producing eggs. After dinner I walked with Annie along a half-mile loop on the property. We did this most days to get some exercise. Annie was almost to term and her walks were getting more and more difficult. Emily trailed behind us with Fescue doing everything but listening to her. The sun was fading into an orange and pink cloudless sky. The breeze was mild, and the temperature was such that a long sleeve shirt was more than enough. I did not want to ruin the perfect night talking about Brooke's case, but I had to mention my plans for the next day.

"I gotta use your Jeep tomorrow to head down to Southfork."

"For what?"

"Brooke's case. There's a long shot we uncovered."

"When you say long shot-"

"I mean a real long shot. But if my road trip gives Sally some peace of mind then it's worth it."

"Will it be dangerous?"

I hadn't thought about risk. It was such a long shot that it never came across my radar. "I don't think so?"

"Brandon, please take someone with you?"

"It's just recon. If it looks plausible, I'll pass a lead on to the FBI to look into it. But as of now I don't want them running down every rabbit hole I uncover. There may come a time when I need them to act on a solid lead and they won't listen if I'm crying wolf every second."

"What time are you planning on going?"

"First thing in the morning."

"Promise you'll be careful."

"Always am," I said, lifting my shirt to reveal my gun in the appendix holster. Annie didn't seem happy with my reply.

NINE

THE NEXT MORNING I WAS UP AT SUNRISE. I POURED A CUP of coffee and packed a small cooler with bottles of water, fruit, and a couple of sandwiches. I left a note addressed to Annie, Emily, Fescue, and John Wayne Hall reminding them that Daddy needed them to drive the property at least once to check on the herd.

As the Jeep warmed up, I emailed JT a note bringing him up to speed on what Drake discovered. I told him that I was driving to Southfork to investigate this contact and not to tell Sally for fear of getting her hopes up. No sooner had I finished the email than a sheriff's car pulled into the driveway and parked next to me. One of my best friends, Jim Tollers, stepped out wearing civilian clothes and a sheriff's baseball cap. His beard, like mine, had started to grey. Jim and I grew up playing baseball together. Tollers received a pitching scholarship to Duke where he proceeded to blow out his arm sophomore year. He dropped out and came back home to recover, eventually becoming a sheriff. Around town he was still referred to as *Fast-Ball Tollers*.

I lowered the window. "And you're here at dawn because?"

"Because I heard from a little birdie that you were going on a road trip without me." He pulled a duty bag out of his back seat and threw it inside the Jeep.

"This little birdie wouldn't be heavily pregnant, would she?"

He smiled, got in the passenger seat and reclined it. "My shift just ended so I'm gonna catch a few z's on the way down okay?"

"Are you sure you-"

He lifted the baseball cap off his face. "After what Annie told me about this case, I'm helping any way I can."

"I'll be gone all day."

"Oh, shut up and drive, Brandon."

"You're unbelievable," I said, putting the jeep into reverse.

He lifted the cap off his head again and smiled. "Do me a favor and remind my wife of that, okay?"

The drive was long, but we hit very little traffic. Tollers slept the entire way. I passed the time listening to scripture from my cell phone via one of my headset buds. The deep voice of Alexander Scourby read First Peter. The theme that jumped out was suffering, and how it was temporary. Having lost my infant son, I knew suffering. My flesh and sin nature kept worrying that Sally was going to experience this same pain. A pain that was indescribable. A drop of water ran down my cheek to wake me from the horrific stroll down memory lane.

A short while later a sign welcomed us to Southfork, Virginia. In the northeastern United States, wealthy towns were located along the coastline. Places like The Hamptons, Providence, and Cape Cod. Virginia was different in that the deeper you went inland the closer you were to the country's capital of Washington D.C. where the greater concentration of wealth was located. Property in Alexandria dwarfed that of coastal places like Hampton and Newport News. Southfork was on the lower income portion of the spectrum. Double-wide trailers and run-down shacks made up most of the main street residential homes with a convenience store, pizza shop, and a garage-sized post office making up the business district.

My paranoia was on high alert since rolling into town. Maybe it was the dark clouds above or the fact that everywhere I looked along the road I saw puddles and marsh revealing how pervasive the swamp was. Misshapen half-rotted trees stood like evil sentinels over the murky water. Somewhere close by was the actual swamp probably filled with snakes and all sorts of nasty creatures. The town would have been the perfect setting for a horror movie.

For some reason the map function on my cell phone could not locate the address. I stopped for gas and a cup of coffee at the convenient store leaving Tollers in the passenger seat. Inside, the young man behind the counter sported a mullet and was struggling to push out what could be referred to as a mustache. I took him seriously when I saw the Glock 17 open-carried on his hip. On the opposite hip was a mid-sized Bowie knife. I placed two coffees on the counter and threw down three bucks.

"Anything else?" He said in a thick southern accent.

"I was wondering if you knew where Dismal Edge Drive was?"

He paused looking me over like I had just said a cuss word. "Why you want to go there?"

"I'm looking at some land?" Which was true, from a certain point of view.

"For what reason?"

I ignored the question. "Do you know the area?"

"You a cop?"

I'd had enough. "You got a problem?"

"We don't like outsiders here."

"I'm a cattle farmer from southern Virginia. If you'd like I can show you my driver's license? I want to go look at some land. Now, do you know the address or not?"

He pointed out the window. "Take a right out of here. Follow it for a couple of miles and you'll see a white church. Right after that is an unmarked dirt road." He smirked, "I'd be careful though."

"Why's that?"

"Jeb Lawson owns most of that section of the swamp and he don't take kindly to people trespassing. I don't know what piece of land you're looking at, but I wouldn't want that fella for a neighbor."

"Understood."

As I turned to leave, he said, "Sorry for my questions. Just a lot of weirdos come through this place."

I pointed to his Glock. "I got that impression by what you carry on your hip. Thanks for the help and sorry for snapping at you."

On the way out I grabbed a free local real estate magazine that was in a wire rack by the entrance. I waited outside the gas station for a few minutes to see if the kid picked up a cell phone to call anyone. He didn't, so I assumed he was telling the truth and was just curious.

When I shut the Jeep door Tollers snoring stopped and he perked up. "Where we at?" he grumbled.

"Southfork. Here's a coffee?" I said handing him the cup.

"Thanks. Did you find the place?"

"It's down the road."

A few minutes later I found the unmarked road. I checked my cell phone again and it had no signal. The entire town seemed to be riddled with cell dead zones. The narrow gravel road had swamp water on both sides and probably flooded on a regular basis. "No Trespassing" signs were nailed to dead trees with rickety branches. After a couple hundred yards, the road forked with the swamp taking up the middle in the form of a small lagoon. The left trail was a bit overgrown and looked as if no one had driven down it in a while. The right side was covered with vehicle tracks.

I continued down the right side and, in a few moments, spied a small cabin with no vehicles parked outside. It was situated on a hill which overlooked the water. Having found an end to this portion of the road, I backed up to where it had forked and drove down it until the gravel turned to mud. Trees and brush blocked the Jeep from going any farther. It looked as if whoever had built the road abruptly stopped. From the moment we turned off the street the cabin was the only real destination along this road.

"Let's go take a look." I said, shutting off the Jeep.

"What am I bringing?" Tollers said, clearly asking if we were going armed or not.

"Bring your Glock," I said.

We left the Jeep and walked back towards the direction of the main road. I checked to confirm my gun's safety was off and that my knife and penlight were both in my pocket. I carried a small rucksack with two spare magazines, binoculars, and small first aid trauma kit for a worst-case scenario. In my hand was the real estate brochures from the gas station. I now had an excuse to approach the house and knock on the door. If someone were home, I'd hand them the brochures and ask if they were interested in listing their river front property. Anything to get into the house to see what was going on.

We reached a spot where we could look over the small lagoon. Across the water and up a grassy hill was a clear view of the cabin. Using the binoculars, I scanned the property. The cabin was small, maybe thirty by thirty with a stove pipe coming out of the side. It was raised on cement footings and had no foundation or basement. The roof was tin with an unmarked satellite dish on it. I took pictures with my cell phone. We observed it for a half hour seeing no movement around the place. I motioned for Tollers to follow me back onto the main road, which continued to skirt the water before climbing the small embankment to end at the cabin's small covered porch. We reached the door and I knocked while Tollers walked off to the side out of sight. There was no answer. The doorknob was locked and had a deadbolt as well.

I moved along the deck to the one dirty window that looked in on the house. From what I could see it was one big open space with a tall ceiling and paddle fan. It was clean and had an old manual hand well pump fitted to a metal countertop beneath the window. It looked like a scene from a western movie. To juxtapose this antique kitchen was a new leather couch opposite a massive flat screen television in the middle of the room. A couple of tables and chairs were interspersed around the space. At the end of the room were single doors on opposite sides of each other. I assumed one was a bedroom and one a bathroom. I stepped off the deck and walked around the perimeter of the house.

Tollers motioned that he'd go around the opposite direction. There were no other windows. I took out my pen light and scanned under the house. There was only one small pipe running up to the kitchen hand-pump and an electric line running into the far side of the cabin. I walked to where one of the back interior rooms were and put my ear to the boards. I knocked on the board-and-batten wood siding, hoping to hear a matching distress response from inside, but nothing happened. I walked to the other side and did the same where the other room was located and received the same results.

Out back behind the cabin was a rusted metal carport with an old truck parked beneath. It looked like it hadn't been run in years. Next to it was a small shed with the door unlatched. Inside was a small battery bank which supplied electricity to the cabin. From this vantage point I could see a few solar panels on the roof of the south-western side of the cabin. Behind me, the property turned into trees and brambles. I walked back around the cabin into the sloping grass front yard heading towards the water. To the right, near a bunch of bushes was a small vent pipe for the septic system. Down at the water's edge was a rickety dock tucked behind vegetation. I had been unable to see it from the opposite shore. A small boat with a v-berth was tied up to a rusted cleat. I stepped on the boat and opened the v-berth to find moldy cushions. I met Tollers back on the porch and tried the door again while he tried the window. Thoughts of breaking-and-entering crossing both our minds. I walked off the deck and around both sides, again listening and knocking. Still nothing.

We headed back in the Jeep where Tollers proceeded to nod off again while I waited for someone to show up. I checked my phone again but there were zero bars on my service. A muffled slap on the driver's side window shook me from the daze. I turned to see the red smear of blood and guts on the door glass. A bloody corpse of a squirrel was slapped into the glass again. The man holding the dead animal also held a rifle in his other hand. He was beefy, bearded, and wore camo hunting clothes. He shouted something and slapped the dead squirrel into the glass a third time. Tollers was awake and outside before me. I pushed the driver's door open forcing the man back.

"What's your problem?" I said, stepping out and keeping my hand near my appendix holster.

He dropped the squirrel and started to raise the rifle. I stepped into his personal space forcing the rifle barrel beyond me. He adapted and started to cock his right fist. I straight jabbed him in the jaw knocking him on his rear. He dropped the rifle, but recovered a moment later lunging for the weapon. I stepped on the barrel making it impossible for him to lift it.

"You're on private property!" he shouted with a thick southern drawl.

"I didn't know," I said. "Regardless, it gives you no right to attack my car or threaten me with a gun." I reached down and grabbed the rifle and tossed it in the water behind him. The swamp seemed to swallow the firearm like a creature being fed a snack.

Tollers stayed on the opposite side of the car hood, his hand under his shirt ready to pull his gun. "You think this is the wild west or something, pal?"

I held up the real estate flyer from the gas station. "I came by to talk to you about land."

He stood up, at least an inch or two taller than me, and probably had twenty pounds on me. "You don't get off my property I'm gonna—"

"You're gonna what, tough guy? Shoot me?"

"I'm gonna make you wish you never seen my face."

"I already regret it," I said.

He rushed me with a fist cocked. I was able to put up my forearm to absorb the hit. I countered with a right to his sternum and hit him with a left in his lower right kidney. The first punch did nothing but the second had an effect. He staggered but was upright a moment later. His eyes glazed over, and he seemed more animal than human as he rushed me again. I could hear Tollers rushing around the Jeep to my aid.

A gunshot went off and everyone stopped.

Another camo clad bearded man exited from the woods behind us. He resembled the same man in front of me and held a similar small caliber rifle. "What you wanna do with em, Jeb?"

"I'd lower your gun," Tollers said, meeting him on the passenger's side of the Jeep. "You have no idea who you're aiming that firearm at?"

This seemed to embolden the young man who walked up and went to use the butt of the rifle to hit Tollers in the chest. In one motion Tollers rolled away pulling the gun and the man toward the Jeep. The hit knocked the wind out of him and within seconds Tollers had the rifle in one hand and his Glock 19 out in the other.

"Here," he said tossing the rifle to me.

I caught it and tossed it into the swamp water to join its partner. The first guy in front of me winced like I had just slapped his child. I could see the absolute fury in his eyes.

Tollers wagged his pistol in the direction of the road. "On your way now fellas?"

The one called Jeb pointed to Toller's gun. "You're here about land huh?"

"You're gonna be in a world of hurt," the second man said, moving away from the Jeep.

Jeb walked back towards the main road. He used his thumb and index to make a gun motion and pretended to shoot us. "I'm gonna find out who you two are."

"I can't tell you how often I've heard that," Tollers said.

In response the man took out a cell phone from his pocket and stopped to take a picture of Annie's license plate. He used his shooting motion fingers again.

After they were far enough away, Tollers said, "What do you want to do?"

"I need to see what's in those rooms in the cabin?"

"Roger that," he said. "I'm gonna call in local PD."

Tollers went into the Jeep and rummaged through his bag. He pulled out a radio and I could hear it chirp to life. While he did that, I checked my cell again. Still no signal. Through the binoculars I watched the two men enter into the cabin.

Tollers got back out of the Jeep. "My radio got through. Local PD is on the way."

We drove the Jeep to the main road and waited for five minutes for a local police cruiser to show up. Tollers got out and showed his badge. After a brief exchange of words, he came back to the Jeep.

"What's the good word?" I said.

"Officer's name is Smith. Seems to be a stand-up guy. Told him we weren't from around here and were threatened and physically assaulted by the two knuckleheads. He wasn't surprised and said that we picked the worst property to drive onto as the two brothers are a nightmare to deal with."

"What did you tell them about our reason we're here?"

"I told him you're a P.I. working on a lead on a case up in Halifax County, and we didn't have enough evidence to go to the cops yet. He understood but said if we wanted to get inside the house, we needed to go the route of a warrant."

"We've spooked them," I said. "If there's any chance Brooke could be in one of those two back rooms, they'd move her by the time we came back with a warrant. We need to get in there today."

"I know, but you gotta follow protocol-"

"Brooke could be in that cabin right now. An arm's

length away from us. We can't walk away."

The young cop came up and knocked on the glass window. Tollers lowered it. "What do you want to do Sheriff Tollers?"

He looked at me then back to the officer. "We need to get in there."

The officer thought for a moment. "Only plausible scenario is if you want to press charges?"

"Could it get you into the house?" I said.

"Not sure," he said. "Depends if they come out?"

"If that's the only way, then we need to press charges."

"It's gonna be a waste of time as you guys were trespassing on private property and, in the end, it will be their word against yours?"

"Understood."

Another cruiser pulled up and Smith went over to talk with the male driver. Tollers got out placing his badge on his shirt. I got out of the Jeep as well.

The second officer, an older male, got out of the cruiser waving his hands back and forth. "Sorry, but I can't bring you with us."

Smith pulled a Kevlar vest from the trunk of his cruiser and handed one to the other officer. "What am I looking for if I get inside the house?"

"There are two side rooms," Tollers said. "We need to know what's in them."

"Are we walking into something dangerous?"

"No," I said. "Just let us know what's inside."

"Want us to get you guys a burger while we're in there?" The older officer said.

"Sorry fellas," I said, not trying not to annoy them further. "We really appreciate it."

Both men drove up to the cabin in one cruiser. Each had their hands on their sidearms as they approached the front door. One pounded on the door while the second stood off to the side. The door opened a crack. Officer Smith talked for a full minute while the second officer looked through the kitchen window with his hand still on his sidearm. Both Lawson brothers stepped onto the porch and closed the door behind them. I could see them pointing towards my Jeep and yelling. Smith held up a hand and shouted something back.

"This ain't going well," I said.

"We may need to step in and help out if this goes south," Tollers said.

A moment later both brothers stepped off the porch and headed towards the cruiser. Each officer handcuffed one brother. Smith stuffed Jeb in the back seat of the cruiser and walked back towards the front door. Just as his partner placed the second brother into the back seat both cuffed men exploded with shouts and tried to push their way back out of the cruiser. It was as if the sight of Officer Smith going towards the front door set them off. As if they had something to hide.

Tollers got out of the Jeep and started towards the house with me following. Both officers were wrestling the handcuffed brothers back into the cruiser. Finally, the car door was shut. From inside the cruiser, the brother's made the vehicle shake like a bunch of football players jumping on the hood. We reached the cruiser just as Smith entered the house.

The older officer held up his hands. "Go back to your vehicle guys. We got this."

We complied and walked back down to the Jeep. My stomach did somersaults with anticipation. The second officer walked up to the front door with his hand resting on his holstered gun. He stood by the entrance shifting his gaze back and forth from the cruiser to the interior of the cabin. Images of Brooke Eldridge flooded my mind. Maybe she was safe and unharmed? It seemed like an eternity before Officer Smith exited alone. Brooke Eldridge wasn't there. It had been a wasted effort. The two officers spoke for at least a minute, then got in the cruiser and drove back down to let Smith out at his vehicle. The other cruiser continued past us with both Lawson brother's shouting at the window in our direction. I assumed it was expletives.

After the cruiser left, I asked Smith, "What did you see?"

"Not much," he said. "Open main living room with nothing in particular. One of the side rooms is a bathroom with a compost toilet. The other room is a small bedroom with two twin beds and some boxes. One closet filled with piles of clothes. There was one bureau with ammo and a few pistols on top. I saw an AR-15 mounted on the wall along with a bolt action. There were a couple of laptops on a small table, but nothing I could legally touch. "

I felt like I had run a marathon. Every ounce of energy drained from my body and I slumped to the ground leaning on the Jeep tire.

"I'm assuming you thought I'd find something else?" he said.

I nodded.

"Sorry I couldn't do more but I'm probably gonna get yelled at for entering the residence in the first place, but I did want to make sure there were no more threats." He held up air quotes when he said the word, *threats*. "Especially, after they resisted arrest."

"I appreciate all you did," Tollers said. "Those laptops-"

Smith waved his hand back and forth. "Don't even go there. You'd need a warrant. Time for you boys to follow me to the station to make a statement. After that, I want you guys gone before you get me fired."

"Thanks again," Tollers said.

TEN

THE SOUTHFORK POLICE STATION WAS A SMALL BRICK building with only a few people working at random desks. Within a half hour Tollers and me had made our statements. We thanked Officer Smith for his help and told him to look us up if he was ever in our part of Virginia.

The older cop was out front smoking a cigarette when we left the building. "Doubtful you guys will have to come back here?"

"Why's that?" Tollers said.

"A fancy lawyer showed up a few minutes ago and is chewing out the chief right now." He pointed to a high-end Mercedes SUV parked diagonally, taking up a guest parking spot and handicapped parking spot. "Charges will more than likely be dropped."

"Sorry for what we put you guys through," Tollers said.

"Clearly you guys are hiding something," he said. "I just hope it was worth it."

Before we left, I took a photo of the Mercedes license plate. Back in the jeep I turned to my friend, "I'm sorry for wasting your time, Tollers."

"Don't say that," he said, reclining his seat and dropping his hat over his eyes again. "My gut tells me we came here for a reason. Those brothers were into something sketchy, even if it has nothing to do with Brooke Eldridge."

"That being?"

"Not sure yet, but were you thinking what I'm thinking?"

"About the lawyer?"

He lifted his hat and nodded. "How the heck does a hillbilly living in a shack in the swamp afford a lawyer who drives a hundred grand Mercedes?"

"What's shocking is how quick he showed up."

"Yup."

Within minutes Tollers was sawing boards again. Poor guy was working on only a few hours sleep. The drive home was quiet with very little traffic, but it was anything but peaceful. I kept replaying every scene in my mind. Both Lawson brothers were hyper-aggressive and brandished their hunting rifles at us. Clearly there was something mentally, and even spiritually, wrong with them, but it didn't mean they were tied to this case. It was just after sunset when I pulled into the farm driveway. Tollers woke up acting like he just had a solid's night sleep.

"When's your next shift?" I said.

He looked at his watch. "About an hour. Enough time for me to go home, take a shower, and change into some clean undies."

"I'm sorry."

He waved his hand. "You've been there for me countless times, Brandon."

Although my friend spoke the truth, I still felt guilty. Inside the house, Annie and Emily sat on the couch with Fescue snoring next to them. The puppy perked up when I entered the room. A moment later she lowered her head and closed her eyes. Annie got up and walked me out to the kitchen. She pulled a plate of steak and rice from the oven. After I said grace and started to eat she hit me with questions on my road trip.

"It was a dead end," I said.

"This guy wasn't on porn sites then?"

"Oh, I'd be willing to bet he's on porn sites, and who knows what else."

"So he's guilty?"

"Of being a complete scumbag yes, but nothing to do with Brooke."

My cell rang. It was JT. I put it on speaker. "How'd your road trip go?"

"You want the bad news or the bad news," I said.

"I want it all," he said.

"We got onto the property and law enforcement was able to get inside his residence, but we found nothing."

"How'd law enforcement get involved?"

I broke eye contact with Annie and lowered my voice as if she wouldn't hear. "We, uh, kind of had an altercation."

"You got in a fight?"

"A little one."

Next to me Annie crossed her arms. "Brandon Hall. You didn't tell me that."

"It wasn't my fault," I said to both JT and Annie. "Cops took care of it."

JT exhaled on the other end of the phone. "Then I got nothing to give to Sally."

"She won't return my calls or texts," Annie added.

"She's in a bad way," JT said. "I'm really worried about her. Please keep her in prayer."

"Anything new from the FBI on your end?"

"Nada."

"Were you able to find anything else from Darren Eldridge's laptop?"

"I've scoured that computer's contents from top to bottom. There's nothing else I can find connecting that one pic of Brooke to anyone else. Are you sure this guy in Southfork is clean?"

"Oh, he's dirty," I said. "I just don't think he has anything to do with Brooke's disappearance. Remember it was a keyword that led us there. Nothing more. We don't know if he was the one who messaged Darren Eldridge. One thing's for sure, if I step foot on that property again, I'll end up with a bullet in my head."

"Thanks for trying, Brandon. I gotta go."

After JT hung up Annie said, "He's never sounded like that before."

"You mean hopeless?" I said. "Reminds me of when I first met him. After his wife left him."

I finished dinner and Annie and I went for a walk around the property with two headlamps on. Her belly had dropped, and she had slowed down to a fast waddle. We passed by the family cemetery plot and Jonah's headstone reminded me that we would soon be a family of four again. After the walk I snuck onto the couch next to Emily. She was asleep with a book next to her. It was one of the Anne of Green Gables novels. On the television the credits rolled for an old black and white film.

I turned to Annie and whispered, "You do realize we have an eighty-year-old for a daughter?"

"She's an old-soul for sure."

"What were you guys watching on tv?"

"Captains Courageous."

I thought about the 1937 nautical movie. "I'm telling you, she may just leave us to go to sea one day."

I carried Emily up to her bedroom like I had done

countless times before. Soon she'd be too big for me to do this. I placed her down in her wrought iron bed and took off her slippers. Annie pulled her matelassé white blanket over her and placed the Anne of Green Gables book on her bookshelf. Next to it were classic cloth-bound books with titles like Nancy Drew and Boxcar Children. I hated that Emily was getting older, but at the same time was excited to see the teenager she'd become.

We walked into the next bedroom. Inside was Jonah's crib along with his toys and decorations. Neither of us could bear to get rid of his toy cars and decorations so we kept everything as it was and chose to change the color from a light blue to a neutral yellow.

"You excited for this room to be filled again?" I whispered.

"I'm nervous placing a new baby in Jonah's crib."

"Don't be superstitious," I said. "We can make new memories with Jonah's crib and toys while respecting the history."

A text appeared on my cell phone from dad. It read, 'Mom's PET scan = stage one. Tumor contained. Prognosis positive. Praise God.'

"Look at this," I said, showing Annie the phone. "Our first new memory in the room."

The exhaustion from the fight with the Lawson brothers coupled with the long drive home finally caught up with me. It was a struggle just to take a shower and crawl into bed. By the time I got out, Annie was asleep and I soon followed.

The next morning I was the first one awake. I let Fescue outside. It was a mild morning, just the way I liked it. In the coming months the heat and humidity would become almost unbearable. Spring was the calm before the proverbial heat storm. As the puppy chased a squirrel towards the barn I went back into the kitchen and took out a cast iron pan to make pancakes. As if they could smell the batter, both my wife and daughter came into the kitchen at the same time.

"Pancakes!" Emily said.

Annie made herself a cup of decaf tea and sat on the front porch to read her daily devotional. I loaded Emily up with pancakes and went out to the porch to bring Annie hers. I joined her with coffee and my flapjacks.

She closed her Bible and picked up her tea. "I was just praying for you."

"For me?" I said.

"I'm worried about you."

"I'm fine."

"You haven't smiled much lately."

"I'm fine," I repeated.

"Brandon, after Jonah died, I thought every breath I took would be my last. You never complained and ignored your pain so you could nurse me back to health. I think some of that pain you pushed down is coming back up."

I took a sip of the strong coffee and let my gaze wander over the property. The cows grazed in incongruent patterns throughout the pastures. It was a peaceful scene compared to what was going on in my brain.

"Brandon, talk to me?"

"Every thought I put into this case physically hurts my mind, my heart, and my soul," I said. "I feel so bad for Sally, and to think Brooke is somewhere right now terrified, or being molested, or even dead makes me want to vomit." My hand instinctively went up to my eye and wiped away the moisture I knew would morph into tears if I kept talking about Brooke. "I'm ashamed to say this, but part of me wishes I never knew Sally, or Brooke. I can't-"

"I think you should take off after church and go fishing with Emily."

"I can't. Mom's surgery is tomorrow."

Annie thought for a moment. "Well, if it goes well then I want you to go fishing on Tuesday."

Fescue jumped up on the porch with a slimy tennis ball in her mouth. Emily came out and picked her up. "How's my baby?"

Annie blurted out. "Emily, if your grandmother's surgery goes well tomorrow your dad's taking you fishing."

Before I could say no, Emily screamed and almost dropped the puppy. I was now committed. The only thing I added was, "Only if Grammy's surgery goes well."

Later that morning Pastor Dale greeted us at church along with the other eighty or so people who attended our small congregation. We sat in the back row next to Mom and Dad. My mother looked like a young forty-something actress from Hollywood's golden era. She seemed unfazed at what lay ahead the next day. The sermon that day was on perseverance. Dale spoke from a myriad of passages about different people in the Bible who persevered through suffering. He brought the message home when he mentioned Brooke by name. Sally and JT sat quietly a few rows up from us. It looked as if he were propping her up. Dale shocked me with how he finished his sermon.

"Romans 8:28 says that God is working in the background for our good. For us believers. Please pray for the FBI and those in law enforcement to solve this crime and to bring Brooke home. Please pray for Sally and JT. In Luke eleven we are told about the persistent neighbor, and in Luke eighteen we're told about the persistent widow. Both are relentless, never giving up, and in the end, both receive justice. I feel like this has been the role apportioned me in all of this. I am praying hourly for Brooke and I believe that God is-," he paused as if a sliver of doubt kept him from saying anything further. "I believe God is working to bring Brooke home."

After church I waited to talk to Dale. He looked tired. Heck, everyone in church looked haggard. The church was small enough that everyone felt some of the pain Sally was going through.

"That was a great sermon," I said, shaking Dale's hand.

"Thanks," he said. "I'm tired of feeling like a victim. People I don't even know are coming to me with horrific statistics and data about Brooke. It's like a spiritual war where the world is sending messages of hopelessness, but I wanted to remind the congregation that God has over-come the world. And when things sometimes seem at their worst is when he surprises us the most. We must have faith."

"You believe what you said on the pulpit?"

"About?"

"About Brooke coming home?"

He paused before he nodded. "I do, Brandon."

"I hope you're right."

Dale grasped my hand again. This time it wasn't a handshake. His grip was firm. "Be in prayer, Brandon. You're going to be needed."

"How?"

He shrugged. "I don't know yet, but your face keeps popping into my mind when I pray. You have a role to play in this."

The rest of the day was quiet. We went to my parents for an early dinner as Mom was not allowed to eat after eight p.m. due to surgery prep. Dad had a fire going in the pot belly wood stove, giving the small cabin a soft warmth that you could feel in your bones. Dad and I prepared grilled chicken over caesar salad. We said grace and I watched my mother eat her dinner like someone who had no worries in the world. Dad kept looking over like she could collapse at any time.

I rested my hand on Mom's arm to get her attention. "You all set for tomorrow?"

"I am," she said, wiping her mouth with a floral napkin before returning it to her lap.

"You worried?"

"Not really." I cocked my head. I didn't believe her. She raised her index finger which meant she was about to preach to me. "Take therefore no thought for the morrow: for the morrow shall take thought for the things of itself."

"Sufficient unto the day is the evil thereof," Emily finished.

"That's right, darling."

I turned to Annie and smiled. I was comforted that Mom quoted me the same scripture Annie quoted when we were in the barn.

"God's got this, Daddy," Emily said.

"Out of the mouth of babes," my dad said, leaning over to kiss Emily on the head.

Early the next morning I drove the farm, checking on the herd. The sun hadn't risen yet and all I could see were dark shapes in the pastures. The fences were fine and nothing seemed out of the ordinary. The cows were munching on spring grass and had plenty of water between the smaller ponds and troughs. After a quick workout and a shower, I was on the road before Annie or Emily woke up. I arrived at Halifax Regional Hospital as my parents checked in. An hour later my dad sat across from me in the cafe. Neither of us spoke much. I knew he was thinking about what the docs were doing to mom.

I broke the silence. "Someday, Emily's generation will

hopefully look back on the way we treat cancer the same way we look back on Civil War medicine."

"I sure hope so. Just the thought of them cutting your mother open makes me want to scream."

"Prognosis is positive, Dad."

"I know," he said taking a sip of coffee. "Tell me something to get my mind off what they're doing to your mom."

"I hit a dead end with the case."

"How so?"

"I thought that I had a solid lead and drove out to the Dismal Swamp to investigate but came up short. It was arrogant of me to think I could figure this out when the FBI is working around the clock with resources beyond anything I could imagine."

"God hath chosen the foolish things of the world to confound the wise."

"First Corinthians," I said. "I'm definitely foolish."

"Don't give up, Son. You're not wasting your time."

We went for a walk outside and came back a half hour later. The doctors had finished up and the kidney had been removed. Initial report was that everything went as well as could be expected. My dad went into recovery to be there when Mom woke. A few hours later, she was admitted to a room and I went up to see her. There were already flowers on the windowsill sent from people at church.

Mom smiled and whispered something. I leaned in closer. "I've been trying to lose those last few pounds. Seems like I got my wish."

I kissed her forehead. "Only you would joke about this." I turned to my dad. "Any more news?"

"Docs said everything's looking good. Gonna hit it with some radiation after she recovers, just to be safe."

Nurses floated in and out throughout the day. I texted

updates to Annie who, in turn, passed along the good news to friends.

Around four o'clock, Jamie came by dressed in casual clothes. "How's my favorite patient doing?"

"You're a dear to visit on your day off," Mom said.

"I heard a rumor that everything went perfect."

"That's right," Dad said, taking up a proud stance next to Mom. He looked like a man whose daughter had just won a spelling bee.

Jamie handed my dad and me each a sheet of paper. "I know you Halls are stubborn, so I took it upon myself to prep meal plans for the next week from people at church."

The sheet in front of me had lunch and dinner breakdowns for both my dad and my family. "Annie and I don't need this-"

Jamie held up her hand. "Shush, Brandon. You're gonna have to be there for your mom and dad. I also know you're working on Brooke's case, and Annie's about to pop. There's no way you're saying no."

"Yes, boss," I said, to the petite generous tyrant.

ELEVEN

It was just before sundown when I pulled into the farm. I sat in the cab of the truck for a few minutes, simply thanking God for delivering my mother from this sickness. I knew she had a long road ahead, but the cancer was contained, and she had a positive prognosis. I felt like I had run a hundred miles, but all I did was sit in a hospital all day. It was amazing how much mental stress affected your physical body. Annie came out to the porch and I walked up to greet her with a hug. I called for Emily who joined us in a group hug to celebrate Mom's good news.

Inside, I ate a couple of pieces of cold pizza and salad. After dinner we took a UTV around the property to check on the herd. Fescue barked from the bed, but the cows didn't seem to mind. A few twinkling stars started to show along with a sliver of moon. A short while later we sat on the porch with a small fire going in the pit just off the deck. We each sipped a cup of chamomile tea and watched Emily teach Fescue how to fetch sticks. That night I had one of the best night's sleep of my life.

The next morning there was an email from Dad on my

cell phone. It was an update on Mom. They eased off her pain killers a bit and she was a little uncomfortable. Otherwise everything was good. I placed Fescue on her line in the yard and joined Annie in her morning devotional on the porch. A slight mist hung over the pastures interspersed with brown splotches from cows giving it an otherworldly appearance. Annie read from Ecclesiastes three.

"To every thing there is a season, and a time to every purpose under the heaven: A time to be born, and a time to die; a time to plant, and a time to pluck up that which is planted; A time to kill, and a time to heal; a time to break down, and a time to build up; A time to weep, and a time to laugh; a time to mourn, and a time to dance; A time to cast away stones, and a time to gather stones together; a time to embrace, and a time to refrain from embracing; A time to get, and a time to lose; a time to keep, and a time to cast away; A time to rend, and a time to sew; a time to keep silence, and a time to speak; A time to love, and a time to hate; a time of war, and a time of peace."

"What made you read from this?" I said.

"Not sure. There seems to be so much good and bad happening at the same time and I've been trying to make sense of it all." She rested a hand on her belly. "We're going through a season of joy, but Sally is going through the worst season of her life since her husband died, and your mom is going through a season of pain."

"I'm going through a season of exhaustion," I added.

"I think you need to take Em fishing and get out of here." I started to say something, but Annie shushed me. "Listen to me, Brandon. This baby could come at any time and your life is going to be chaotic for months after that. I'm gonna need you to help with homeschooling and around the house as well as your day-to-day farm responsibilities. Your mom is going to need help as well." I started to say something again and she held up her hand again. "Shut up and listen."

"Did you just tell me to shut up?"

She laughed. "You've done everything you can for Sally. Keep thinking and don't give up, but you need to get out of here for a few hours. As much as you love the farm, I know you can't relax here as you always see work that needs to be done. I know how much you love fishing, and you need to spend time with your daughter before the baby comes. Once he's here it's gonna be chaos and Emily won't get as much one-on-one time with either of us."

"You keep saying the baby is a he."

"If it's a he," she clarified. "Are you even listening to me?"

I had and couldn't think of a reason to counter her argument. Emily strode out onto the porch in her bathrobe and immediately went to pick up the puppy.

When she came back Annie said, "Your dad's taking you fishing today."

Emily's eyes went from half asleep to almost popping out of her head. "Can we go to Smith Mountain Lake?"

"After I stop by to see your grandmother first."

"Can I please bring Fescue?"

"Untrained puppies don't belong on boats," I said. "Maybe when she gets a little older."

"Okay, when can we leave?"

"I'm gonna drive the property and go to the hospital. I'll be back by nine, and we can be on the lake by lunch if we hurry."

Emily ran inside without a word. Annie got up and we walked hand in hand out towards the main pasture. We did our small loop. She stopped a few times to hold her belly when the baby kicked. I placed my hand on her stomach. It was amazing to feel a little leg press up against her skin. He, or she, was only a few inches away yet miles away at the same time. The child was comfortable and safe and had yet to feel the sting of life. I prayed for a quiet, peaceful future. We continued to walk and the guilt I felt about leaving the farm, Brooke's case, and my mom lifted off my shoulders and I knew it was okay to take a break.

When I got to the hospital, Mom seemed tired. A nurse had just made her get out of bed and walk the floor. They wanted to make sure she was functioning at a normal level before they would discharge her. I told Dad about taking Emily fishing, and was half-expecting him to tell me about a farm need, but he was adamant that it was a great idea.

On the ride back home, I called JT to check in. His voice was hoarse like he hadn't slept. "Hey Brandon."

"Any word from the FBI?"

"Same daily message. They still have Brooke's case as a priority, blah, blah, blah. They've offered the guy in custody, Jeffers, a couple of sweet deals, but he keeps giving them nothing."

"How's Sally?"

"She's bad. If the worst case happens and they find Brooke-" he stopped and cleared his throat. "Her husband's death almost killed her, but this will finish the job."

"JT, I'm at a loss and praying for a miracle."

"Keep thinking, Brandon. Please keep thinking."

When I pulled up to the house, Emily was already out front wearing her beige floppy fishing hat and her matching fishing vest. Fescue was swatting a bobber hanging off the end of her fishing pole. I backed into the barn where I kept a small seventeen-foot center-console boat. I picked the boat up at an estate sale a few years back. She was old and ugly but did the job of getting me on the water when needed. I hooked up the boat trailer and threw two jerry cans of gas into the truck bed along with my fishing pole. Inside the house were frozen leftover fish we kept in the freezer for bait. I traded my cowboy boots for boat shoes and grabbed a Red Sox baseball cap JT had given me. Annie had packed us a lunch and walked me back out to the truck. Emily handed Fescue's leash to Annie.

"Make sure your dad relaxes and has fun," Annie said, before kissing me goodbye.

"Don't worry about us," I said.

No sooner were we on the road that my energetic eleven-year-old said, "Water's warm enough. Maybe we can do some water skiing after we fish?"

"We'd need a third person in the boat to spot the skier while I drive." I added, "What did I tell you to work on?"

"I know. Stay in the moment."

"Let's focus on fishing and not the next thing. Enjoy every moment because in a flash your life could change, and in a flash, you'll be an adult."

"Sorry, I'm just excited and want to do everything."

"I know, baby. I love your enthusiasm." I pointed out the window. "So, I spy with my little eye something blue."

Emily perked up and started clapping her hands at our driving game. "Is it the sky?"

"Nope."

"Is it inside or outside the truck?"

"Not telling."

An hour and a half later we reached Smith Mountain Lake. It was a higher elevation and had mountain water running into it, so the clarity was much better than the murky farm ponds and clay bottom lakes we were used to. It was early enough in the season that the boat ramp was empty. Within a half hour I had the boat in the water, the truck parked, and was gunning the old Evinrude engine.

My daughter named the boat Daisy. The joke being that due to the boat's age she'd soon be pushing up daisies.

The engine put out a bit of smoke but ran well enough. Emily stood next to me holding onto her hat with a smile on her face. Whenever I looked over, she kept giving me the thumbs up to go faster. I drove around for a half hour getting the cobwebs out of the motor before finding a deep spot that had provided us with catfish in the past. I cut the engine and Emily knew to drop the small anchor at the bow. Above, the few clouds in the sky couldn't seem to decide what they wanted to do. Some were grey while others a puffy white as they lazily crossed the heavens. I checked my phone and realized the area was set to get hit with thunderstorms later in the day.

I showed the phone to Emily. "Looks like we may only get an hour or two in before it rains."

"We can still fish in the rain."

"I have ponchos on board, but if it turns into a thunderstorm, we gotta call it a day, okay?"

"Okay," she said. "Here, I baited the hooks." She handed me a rod with the right size hook and weighted correctly for catfish.

"You're a pro," I said tossing the line over the side.

Emily dropped her line over. I took out the sandwiches and gave one to Emily along with a bottle of water. After we said grace I fished on the stern bench while she did the same at the bow. We both seemed to exhale at the same time.

"Enjoy this moment, sweetie."

"I am, Daddy."

If I focused hard enough I could still see some of the childlike cuteness in her face. Yet she was more teenager now than a child. The chubby cheeks were giving way to cheekbones and the cute squinty eyes were now beautiful deep-set brown almond eyes. I silently thanked God for this time with Emily. As if in answer to my prayer a thought floated into my mind of friends who worked in big cities. They could never, at the last minute, take a random Tuesday off to go fishing with their kids without filling out triplicate forms to be approved by some white-collar manager.

I thought about the child in Annie's belly and tried to picture all four of us on the boat as a family. I didn't care if the baby was a boy or girl. At that moment I was at peace and overwhelmed with joy.

Emily had a tug on her line, and she squealed, "I think I got something."

"Reel it in!"

She struggled with the rod. It bent to the point of almost breaking. It was a big fish.

I rushed to the bow to help her, but she pushed my hand away. "I got it."

As a dad, my first reaction will always be to help her, but I knew she needed to do things on her own. A moment later the line snapped. She huffed and stomped her right foot. Without looking at me she pulled out the tackle box and started to thread another hook without complaining.

"That's my girl."

An hour later we had two five-pound catfish in the boat's hold. Above us the sky had darkened but the wind was now eerily calm. Specks of rain teased us. I checked the weather on my cell phone and the timetable for the thunderstorms had moved up.

"We should think about heading in," I said.

"It's not even raining," Emily said.

"I should at least move back towards the boat ramp," I said. "That way if it turns into a downpour, we can get out quick."

The wind picked up and the smell in the air brimmed with a clean ozone scent I associated with thunderstorms. The clouds were now moving rather than simply floating. I finished pulling up the anchor and the drizzle turned to rain. There was a dim lightning flash overhead but no thunder to accompany it.

"See," I said. "Storm's coming."

Emily's fishing rod bent. "I think I got something?"

"Good job. Now reel it in, baby."

A boom exploded overhead which sent me to the deck. Emily dropped her rod and would have crawled into my shirt if she could have. Lightning flashed overhead followed by another explosion of thunder, which echoed throughout the lake.

"Sit down, sweetie," I said, moving to the console to fire up the engine. It turned over but wouldn't start. "Come on."

Emily's eyes widened and she tried to reach for my hand. Unfortunately, it was my turn to push her hand away. I needed both of them to fire up the engine.

"Daddy?"

"It's fine, baby."

Both the wind and waves started to pick up. There was another flash and boom overhead. Within seconds the sky had darkened to the point it looked like night. I had never witnessed a shift in weather this extreme and this fast. Emily reached for her rod to finish reeling in the fish.

A long, steady alert chirped on my phone. The last time this alert went off was in Richmond when Brooke went missing. The morbid sound had always made me nervous, but since Richmond its impact increased a hundredfold. The alert meant one of two things. A weather warning or Amber Alert. It was clear this time which it was for. I checked the phone. It was a tornado warning for Bedford,

Franklin, and Pittsylvania counties which surrounded Smith Mountain Lake.

"Cut the line," I said.

Emily did as she was told. The boat was tossed back and forth like a toy in a bathtub. Water splashed over the gunwale. Dark shapes that looked more like demons than clouds raced overhead faster than I thought possible. The bilge pump was going crazy trying to expel the incoming water.

"Daddy, what's happening?"

"Bad storm, sweetie. Gotta head back to the boat ramp." The engine finally turned over. "Thank you, Lord."

"I'm scared."

I couldn't lie to her. Instead, I said nothing and gunned the throttle. A wave splashed over the gunwale and soaked Emily, but she didn't complain. The engine screamed every time we crested a wave and the prop partially came out of the water. There was no way we'd make it back to the boat ramp. I had to get to the nearest shoreline which was still a good quarter mile away.

Emily snuggled up next to me shivering. "Daddy?"

"Pray baby," I said, looking skyward. "Father, I trust you."

As if to counter my prayer, a massive wave hit us broadside and swamped the boat. Water was now over my ankles. Emily started crying. The boat somehow still inched us towards the shore. Lighting flashed with gaunt ethereal bolts and thunder drowned out the straining boat engine. The vibration under my feet ended. The engine had stalled, the boat was swamped, and we were dead in the water.

Emily looked to me with terror in her eyes. "Daddy, what are we gonna do?"

"I don't know baby," I shouted.

There was movement onshore. Through periodic light-ning flashes I could see trees being sucked up into the sky. A tornado had touched down. Emily cried out, but I could no longer understand what she was saying over the wind, rain, and thunder, only that her grip on my waist got tighter. I kept praying for God to show me a way. We needed a miracle. I crouched down in the shallow water and covered Emily with my body. The waves rocked the boat like a giant hand playing with a bathtub toy. More water swamped the boat.

We weren't going to make it.

TWELVE

THE SOUNDS OF EXPLODING TREES ONSHORE REMINDED ME of mortars going off from my time in the Marines. I had never felt this helpless in my entire life. No, there was one other time. When I held the lifeless body of my infant son. The memory of him was replaced by a picture of Emily.

I kept repeating in Emily's ear, "I got you, baby," as we sat in the cool water.

My daughter begged me to make it stop. I realized just how helpless I was and I, in turn, called out to my Father. I couldn't hear my voice, but I knew God could. "Help us, Lord."

The wind created massive waves that continued to hammer the boat. Thunder exploded directly above us. In the distance a bolt of lightning struck the lake. It felt like we were in the middle of a heavenly firefight. How would death come? Would it be quick and violent, or would we suffer?

From under the stern bench a small youth 50 cubic foot scuba tank floated out into the knee-deep water. A remnant from last fall when I taught Emily how to scuba dive. I grabbed the tank and realized by its weight there was minimal air left in it. It was enough to help us escape in the only direction available. I reached under the center console where I kept a spare regulator. I had to pry Emily off me to put the tank together. I grabbed two masks from the same spot under the console and handed one to Emily.

"What are we doing?" she cried.

"Trust me, baby." She nodded and I repeated as loud as I could, "Do you trust me?"

"Yes, Daddy," she said, shivering from either being soaked, or afraid, or both.

"We gotta go down to get away from this."

I rushed to the bow and tossed the anchor overboard. I placed the mask around my neck and made sure Emily's mask was secure on her face. The boat was no longer being thrown around as it was completely filled with water. I lowered Emily over the side where she instinctively grasped onto the taut anchor line. I took a last glance towards shore. It was dark with intermittent lightning followed by massive explosions. Slowly, the flickering outline of the tornado came into focus. Through flashes of lightning it towered over a barn perched on a hill. A moment later the barn was gone, completely obliterated.

"Lord in Heaven."

I turned on the air tank and jumped over into the water. I stuck the regulator in Emily's mouth and pointed my thumb downward. She dropped below the surface and I followed with the tank in hand. She knew to use the anchor line as a means to pull herself deeper into the safety of the lake. I touched her leg to let her know to stop so I could raise the mask up over my face and purge the water from it. I handed her the tank to hold while I did this. A moment later we swapped back. Emily handed me the backup octopus regulator so I could take a breath. We lowered ourselves down a few more feet. Emily knew to equalize pressure in her ears by pinching her nose and trying to blow out at the same time. I did the same before motioning for her to keep going deeper.

As far as I knew, no human had ever survived a tornado this way, but I figured the greater the depth underwater the greater our odds of survival were. At this depth the water was cold, but our air would run out before hypothermia would set in. Somewhere around twenty-five feet I motioned for Emily to stop. I held onto the anchor line and her with one arm while keeping the small tank tucked under my other arm. The gauge read about five minutes of air left. With two of us that would be cut in half. I kept thinking how this is what it might have been like floating in my mother's womb. Safe, and protected while the storms of life raged on outside, but I had no idea if we were, in fact, safe or protected.

Suddenly, the anchor line jerked like a fishing line that caught the biggest tuna in the world. A moment later it was ripped from my hand as the boat was pulled away from above us. The water in front of me darkened as blood from the rope burn on my palm mixed in. I let go and watched the line whisk away like a kite carried off by the wind. I pulled Emily away from the line just before the anchor rushed past us towards the surface of the water. Nature had flexed its muscles, and the amount of violent raw power was unbelievable. Even at this depth I could feel the water stirring as it moved us side to side. I took another breath of precious air. The gauge read that we were almost out, and I was burning oxygen trying to stay in a neutrally buoyant position.

I made the decision to leave Emily with the remainder of the air. If I stayed, then we would both be forced to surface too soon. Regardless of what would happen to me she was a good swimmer and should be able to reach the shore. I took one last breath and motioned with my hands for her to stay down. She shook her head back and forth as if she knew what I had resigned myself to do. I handed her the tank and put my hand to my lips in a mock kissing motion before resting it on her head. A moment later I started my ascent.

At fifteen feet, the water moved like a jacuzzi on steroids. Within seconds I'd surface and be ripped to shreds. I paused and prayed, not for deliverance but for the strength to face the storm waiting for me on the water's surface. The moment passed and my lungs were on fire forcing me towards air and what I knew was death. As I approached the surface a light began to shine above. It reminded me of stories I read of people who suffered near death experiences. Many times the stories mentioned seeing a light before they were resuscitated. A peace washed over me, and there also seemed to be a stillness within the water. For some reason my last thoughts turned back to calm waters of the Dismal Swamp. I swam the last few feet and broke the surface of the lake gasping for air.

Above me the sun blazed in a near cloudless sky and the waves were a fraction of what they were moments earlier. I lifted the mask onto my forehead. In the distance Daisy half-floated in two pieces spread out a hundred yards apart. The shore looked like a nuclear blast had decimated the entire landscape, but the tornado was gone.

"Thank you, Lord," I said.

I placed the mask back on and dove underwater to go after Emily but was greeted by a line of bubbles. A moment later Emily swam past me and surfaced. I resurfaced and treaded water next to her.

She let go of the tank and took off her mask. "Are you okay Daddy?" she said, her lip shivering.

"Why didn't you stay down there?"

"I was worried about you."

"You're so stubborn," I said, spitting out water.

"Just like my dad," she said, also spitting water out.

Tears flowed from my eyes mixing with the lake water. I thanked God for the miracle at the last minute. "C'mon, we gotta get to shore before we freeze out here."

As we swam towards shore the shock of the miracle started to sink in. How the small spare scuba tank appeared at the exact moment we needed, with the exact amount of air we needed? God never failed to surprise me, but I couldn't help but wonder if there was another reason for the rescue?

We crawled onto the shore shivering. I worried Emily might be in shock or suffering from hypothermia. We were far from civilization and the boat ramp where I had parked the truck. I emptied out my pockets on the ground. The only items I had on me were a useless soaked cell phone, a wallet, my pocket knife, pen light, and my keychain which had a whistle, and a small ferrocerium rod attached to it. Emily had her knees up to her chin and looked paler than usual. I dug around and was able to find a few dry leaves, dead pine needles, and dead twigs. My hands shook as I used the pocketknife to cut the twigs into small shavings. The outside of the twigs were slightly wet but once the bark was removed the insides were dry. I mixed the shavings with the crumpled leaves and pine needles.

"What are you doing?" Emily said, shivering.

"We gotta raise our body temperatures up."

I struck the ferro rod with the ninety-degree spine of the knife blade and sparks flew into the small bird's nest of shavings. A spark took and I blew on it to add oxygen. A beautiful red-orange flame appeared and one-by-one I added more twigs and pieces of dried dead limbs scattered about.

"Good job, Daddy," Emily shivered.

Soon, we had a small fire warming us. I took off my boat shoes and made Emily place her sneaks and socks by the fire. We alternated our hands close to the fire with our feet. I cut a piece of my shirt and wrapped it around the palm of my hand where the rope cut me.

Around us there was a handful of medium-sized oak and hickory trees standing like leafless sentinels in an otherwise desolate wasteland. No birds chirped and the sun acted as if nothing happened out of the ordinary. I snuggled next to Emily to try to keep her body temperature up.

"Did I ever tell you how I met your mom?" I said, rubbing her shoulders to make sure the blood flowed.

"At the Halifax County Fair?"

"Yeah, we were both freshmen in high school. She came from a homeschool background, so we had never met before. Tollers introduced me to her as he was trying to woo one of her girlfriends. Your mom was so shy, and I couldn't tell if she even liked me." I paused to make sure Emily was paying attention and not going into shock. "I mean, come on. What woman wouldn't find me attractive?" Emily laughed. She was fine. We were fine. I thanked God again.

An hour later I said, "Are you ready to start the hike back to the truck, if it's even there?"

"I'm ready."

"Your mom's gonna blow a gasket if she doesn't hear from us soon."

Emily held my hand as we walked through what was left of the woods back onto the highway. The squishing sounds from our wet shoes were the only noise in the desolate forest. Eventually, a police cruiser with lights flashing pulled over.

"You're an answer to a prayer," I said.

"What happened?" The young male officer said.

"Got caught out on the lake in our boat. We survived, but the boat didn't."

"Where you heading?"

"Penhook boat ramp at Smith Mountain Lake."

"Get in."

We both squished into the front seat. The officer put the heat on high and I felt like a piece of frozen meat thawing by the second. His radio kept chirping from different officers, headquarters, and EMS. He answered all requests for assistance by stating he would be there as soon as possible.

When there was a lull in the radio calls I said. "How bad is it?"

"As of now there're three people missing," he said. "Elderly couple and a single male. Governor has already declared a state of emergency. Property damage is off the charts. Never seen anything like this."

We reached the boat ramp and found my truck intact. This side of the lake only received rain and wind.

"I can't thank you enough," I said to the officer, "but I need one more favor. I'd like to let my wife know we're safe."

He handed me his personal cell phone. I dialed Annie who picked up on the first ring. "Annie, we're fine-"

"Oh, thank the Lord," she said. "I got the text alert and have been trying to call you nonstop. Are you both okay? What phone are you calling from?"

"My cell is a bit waterlogged. I'm borrowing a cop's cell phone and can only talk for a minute."

"What happened?"

I told her the truth but left out the scary parts. "Uh, we got caught in the storm, but the tornado missed us. We're fine. Will be home soon. I gotta give the phone back to the officer."

After I hung up the young officer smiled. "You glossed over a few things."

"No need to worry the wife," I said. "So, what's the protocol for my boat floating around Smith Mountain Lake? I'm not gonna get fined?"

He shrugged his shoulders. "This is unprecedented and the least of my concerns. Just get home safe and we'll deal with your boat later."

Emily went around to the driver's side to give him a hug and I gave him a wet business card from my soaked wallet in case he needed me to fill out paperwork for the boat. I kept an emergency bag in my truck with first aid and extra clothes for the entire family. I made a mental note to add diapers and newborn outfits into the bag after I got home. Within minutes we were dry and the heat was going in the truck. I cleaned and bandaged the palm of my hand with the first aid kit.

The drive out of Smith Mountain Lake was surreal. Homes, barns, and properties were utterly razed. I had to swerve into the opposite lane to avoid debris spread along the road, much of which was vegetation and animal carcasses from surrounding farms. Emily remained stoic.

"You okay, birthday girl?"

"Yeah. I just can't believe what I'm seeing. It reminds me of that end of world sci-fi movie we watched. All these people's homes are gone."

We passed by a home that had been spared but their barn was ripped in half. A young couple wandered around the property with confused looks on their faces.

"Remember Em, homes can be replaced, lives cannot."

Twenty minutes later we turned onto route 501 and it appeared as if nothing had ever happened. The roadway was busy, gas stations were full, and people pulled into drive-thru fast food restaurants. The damage, like storms and war, had limits, and we had crossed a type of demilitarized zone back into civilization.

Throughout the remainder of the drive, I kept replaying over and over the miracle God provided to let us escape the storm. I was obsessive about my scuba gear cleanliness, maintenance, and storage. How could I forget a tank on the boat? And why would it float out at the last second like an exclamation point from God? It was clear He had spared us, but somehow, I felt like it was a two-fold message.

It was eight o'clock when we pulled back into the farm. Annie was sitting in a rocking chair on the porch. She rushed over and hugged Emily. She pushed her away to an arm's length and scanned her for injuries.

"We're fine Mom," Emily said, like it was no big deal.

Annie pointed to my bandaged hand. "What happened?"

"Small cut."

She then pointed to the empty boat trailer attached to the truck. "Where's the boat?" I shrugged and winced knowing I was about to get a tongue-lashing. "You told me the storm missed you." She said, her voice rising.

"It did," I said.

Emily proceeded to tell Annie about our scuba diving adventure. I walked my wife over the porch steps and motioned for her to sit down. I kept repeating the words, "breathe" and "remember the baby", but her stare told me she wasn't happy with my original version of the story.

In bed that night Annie latched onto me like a child who had woken from a nightmare and didn't want to fall back asleep. I reminded her that we were fine and that the storm was a fluke.

"I know, but I would have died if something happened to you two."

I pointed to the ceiling paddle fan rotating in rhythmic circles above us. "I honestly don't remember leaving that tank in the boat. God performed a miracle but-" I paused. "I feel like there's another message I need to decipher."

"Like what?"

"Not sure yet. I'm working through it."

The next morning, I woke before sunrise. I worked out in the small gym in the barn. Forty minutes later I was in my rocking chair on the porch with a cup of coffee and a bowl of oatmeal. I kept replaying the storm scenario over-and-over in my mind. Was it a random act of nature that I was caught up in? A sign from God? A warning? All of the above? The scuba tank hidden on my boat was the lynchpin showing me it was more than a random coincidence. The supernatural was at work in this. I spent the next fifteen minutes in prayer, but nothing came to me.

Annie joined me on the porch with a cup of herbal tea. She handed me a certified letter. "I had to sign for this yesterday."

I opened it and read through a form letter. "It's a restraining order saying I can't step foot on Jeb Lawson's property in Southfork again without going to prison." I pointed to the law firm who represented Jeb in court. "You ever hear of Dwight and Skuggs?"

"No, but you should send this along to JT. He has lawyers who can deal with this-"

"I don't want to bother him." I picked up Annie's cell phone and looked up the law firm. The website did not say much, but did give an address for their main office. I tucked the piece of paper into my shirt. "I gotta go into

South Boston to get a replacement cell phone. I'm going to continue on to Clarksville."

"What's out there?"

"Senator Schilling told me to stop by his estate if I was around." I tapped my shirt where the paper was. "This law firm is based out of Alexandria, Virginia. His neck of the woods. Maybe he knows something about them?"

"I thought you said this entire thing was a dead end?"

"I just want to turn over this one last stone."

THIRTEEN

SOUTH BOSTON WAS A SMALL CITY COMPARED TO PLACES like Danville or Richmond, but I still felt claustrophobic whenever I drove through. I waited for a half hour at my cell phone provider just so I could pay an exorbitant deductible to replace my waterlogged phone. The drive from South Boston into Clarksville along route 58 was a peaceful contrast to the congestion I had just left. The scenic road gradually rose up to meet the clear sky. I passed very few stores and what seemed like endless farms. Much had changed during my lifetime in Virginia while much had stayed the same.

The small town of Clarksville sat on the shores of Buggs Island Lake, the largest lake in Virginia. A few blocks behind Virginia Drive in downtown was a massive estate. The long gravel driveway was lined with magnolia trees.

The white antebellum home had Georgian columns at the entrance. I parked my truck next to a shiny 1920s Ford model-T. The nine-plus decade old vehicle looked like it had just rolled off the assembly line while my newer 1976

F250 pickup looked like a patchwork job from a junkyard. The two contrasting vehicles were a reminder that I had stepped from one world into another. I straightened my untucked shirt and fixed my jeans which were bunched up over my right cowboy boot. In the truck mirror, my hair was in a semi-combed form and my beard wasn't too unruly. Had I thought through this better I'd have worn khakis and a nice button-down shirt.

At the grand entrance the oak door opened just as I raised my hand to knock. Senator Gregory Schilling, a four-term senator, stood just over six feet and was dressed in a navy-blue pinstripe suit complete with a silk hankie neatly folded in his breast pocket. His salt-and-pepper hair, tan complexion, and big smile looked more Hollywood than Washington D.C.

He grasped my hand in a firm shake. "Good to see you, Brandon."

"You too, sir."

"Come inside."

Stepping into the house was like being transported back into multiple eras at the same time. From the 1800s up to the 1930s. The marble foyer was as big as both my kitchen and living room combined. A wrought iron elevator ascended through the middle of a grand spiral staircase up to a second story landing.

"I gotta bring my wife with me next time," I said. "She'd love this architecture."

"Your family is welcome anytime." He gestured to a room off to the left. "I was just about to have coffee in the library."

We entered what looked like the Library of Congress. It was lined with floor-to-ceiling wood bookcases packed with leather-bound antique books. A brass ladder was linked to a track above the bookcases, which allowed you to reach the top shelves. Bronze busts of old men lined a mahogany table, and original antique oil paintings were mounted to the walls with thin brass picture lights over them.

I waved my free hand around the library. "My daughter would live in this room if she could."

"It's my favorite place in the house," he said. "This home is one of the only places in the world I feel at peace. When I come here from D.C. it's like a switch goes off and I can breathe."

"I've only been to Washington a half dozen times in my life. I couldn't get out of there fast enough."

"I enjoy the city life as well as country living, but over the past few years I'm spending less and less time up there. I think I'm getting too old."

An elderly woman dressed all in black brought a silver platter into the library and placed it down on a marble top coffee table. She saw me and produced a second china cup and saucer from a nearby glass case.

"Anything else, Senator?"

"No, thank you, Sophie." The Senator said. He motioned towards a gorgeous leather couch. "Brandon, come sit with me for a minute."

We faced a lit fireplace that smelled of cedar logs. The Senator poured us each a cup of coffee from a sterling pot. I added a dash of milk and took a sip of the rich coffee.

"Brandon, how's your wife and daughter?"

"Everyone's good," I said. "Annie's about to pop with our third."

"Your third?" He said, surprised. The Senator's eyes darted back and forth as if he were doing a mental tally. "Oh, your son. I'm sorry, Brandon."

I raised my hand to disarm his guilt. "Senator, don't beat yourself up. We've both lost sons."

His eyes filled up at the mention of his boy. He reached out and grasped my hand. "You helped bring my family closure during the worst time of our lives. To you, it may have been just another case, but it's a debt we can never repay."

"It was more than just a case for me."

The sad moment passed, and the Senator's smile returned. His cell phone vibrated from a breast pocket in his suit jacket. He reached his hand inside the jacket and quickly silenced it. "Sorry about that."

"Senator, if you need to take a call, by all means-"

"I'm sure it's just a donor looking for a favor. I can get back to them." He poured himself more coffee. "So what can I help you with?"

"How do you know I need help with something?"

He patted the pocket that held his cell phone. "I'm a politician. I have a sixth sense on these things."

I grinned like a child caught in the proverbial cookie jar. "Now that you mention it, I would like to pick your brain for a minute?"

"Of course."

"I'm working on a case in Southern Virginia and had an altercation on a random property."

He grinned. "An altercation, huh?"

"This guy I got in a fight with is a complete scumbag, but probably not related to the case. However, I wanted your opinion on something before I shut the book on him." I took out the restraining order document and handed it to the Senator. "By any chance, do you recognize this law firm, Dwight and Skuggs? They're out of Alexandria."

The Senator's eyes widened but he didn't say anything. He read the document with one finger going line-by-line. When finished, he folded it, and returned it to me. "D-and-

S are pit bull lawyers who do side work for an organization called the North American Poverty Law Group."

"Never heard of 'em."

"They're the pro bono subsidiary of Global Poverty Law Group."

"Never heard of them either."

"The financier behind the global outfit is our mutual friend Gaspar Schultz."

Gaspar Schultz was a billionaire who manipulated markets and helped finance coups in third world countries in an effort to facilitate open-borders and a one world government. The man was a devil who funded everything from abortion clinics to anarchist groups. Senator Schilling's late son Drew got involved in a group funded by Gaspar Schultz and was murdered because of the affiliation.

"I've been after Schultz since Drew's-" He gritted his teeth as if he were using every ounce of willpower not to cry. "I've run across D-and-S lawyers, along with dozens of other law firms Schultz works with. Can you tell me about the case you're working on? Is it more anarchist college groups?"

Because it was such a high-profile case there wasn't much information I needed to hold back regarding Brooke's abduction. At the end of the story the Senator rubbed his temples like he was fending off a migraine.

"That's a horrific story, Brandon."

"I came here convinced this guy, Jeb Lawson, was not involved, but now that he has loose ties with Gaspar Schultz via his lawyers, I'm starting to second guess it. The million-dollar question is, do you think Schultz could be involved in human trafficking?"

"It wouldn't surprise me." The Senator rose and walked over to a window. On the other side of the glassed pane a mockingbird and cardinal fought over something in the branches of a maple tree. "The more I learn about Schultz, and the circles he travels, the more horrified I become."

I joined him at the window. Outside, the birds flew away. The sun had fallen behind a massive grey cloud. I couldn't tell if it was a temporary passing cloud, or if it would turn to rain.

"I wish more people in positions of power would wake up to fight evil men like Schultz."

"It took the death of my son to wake me up." After a pause he said, "I've found that politicians are either complacent or compromised."

"What do you mean?"

"Since starting my quest to bring Schultz to justice I've hit every roadblock imaginable. Most of which was deliberately placed in my way. I believe Schultz, and the deep state, has infiltrated both parties in Congress. Even some of the circuit court judges and possibly a few of the Supremes." He exhaled and seemed to hunch over like an old man. "I must confess, that some days, the enemies of the Constitution seem too powerful to overcome." He turned from the window. "In the end, I don't think the good guys will win this fight, Brandon."

"I can do all things through Christ, which strengthenes me."

"What was that you said?"

"A passage from Philippians."

The Senator's demeanor softened. "We could use some help from the Almighty."

I left the meeting with Senator Schilling more confused than before I showed up. Jeb Lawson was more than likely a violent scumbag who liked to surf child porn. That didn't make him a child abductor or someone who dealt in human trafficking. The Dwight and Skuggs lawyers loosely tied him to Schultz and his billions, but it wasn't damning evidence. Nothing I had would hold any weight in a court of law, nor would it even perk the FBI's interest. It was still too thin.

I arrived back at the farm to find Moss Burnell parked in his brother's pickup truck by the barn. I walked over to greet Colt's youngest brother. Sitting next to him was a familiar young lady wearing a blue and white gingham dress with her bare feet up on the dashboard.

"Well, hello, Mossberg. Your brother still on his honeymoon?

"Yup, he's loving Nashville."

"So, what can I do for you two?"

"I wanted to take you up on your offer to fish your pond."

"Of course," I said. "The fish are already biting." I reached beyond Moss to shake the young lady's hand. "I think we met at the wedding but your name slips my mind?"

"Minnie."

"Nice to see you, Minnie."

"So, Moss told me some crazy story about how you all met," she spoke quick and full of energy. "A government conspiracy and a murder? Is that all true?"

I waved my hand. "Moss likes to be a little dramatic at times. Truth is Moss and me both had the same probation officer."

I walked away and could hear Moss trying to explain that I was joking. He kept calling after me to come back and tell the truth. I waited a good minute before rejoining them and validating Moss' story.

The three of us walked down the dirt road to the main pond where I proceeded to show them the best fishing spots. Above us, the sun was set in a semi-clear sky. By the warm breeze I could tell it was around eighty degrees. Summer was fast approaching. Before leaving I ventured to ask Moss a question. I knew the Burnell brothers were Christians and thought a fellow believer might have some insight as to what happened to me. I gave him an abbreviated version of Brooke's case and the Smith Mountain Lake story but made sure to include the miraculous underwater escape. When I finished Moss shrugged his shoulders and mumbled something about prayer, but it was Minnie who surprised me.

"Have you searched scripture, Mr. Hall? I'm certain you'll find your answer."

"I hadn't," I said, realizing that besides prayer, that was where I should have looked. I smacked Moss in the chest. "Moss, you got a good one here. Don't mess it up."

Minnie blushed, "You listen to Mr. Hall, Mossberg." She handed Moss a rod with a baited hook.

He didn't respond to her statement. Instead he said, "Did you pack the lunches?"

"Yes. And before you ask, yes I cut the crust off your sandwich."

"Seriously?" I said. Moss showed no signs of shame or embarrassment. "Minnie, you got a real momma's boy on your hands."

"Tell me about it," she said, "and I enable it."

Back on the porch I sat in a rocking chair and rifled through a worn bible for anything that might jump out at me. I started my search with stories of God rescuing people in fantastical ways. From Peter being freed from prison by an angel, to Daniel in the lion's den, to the many times Paul escaped death. Eventually, it was the watery shipwrecks of Paul which struck a chord. It reminded me of our shipwreck at Smith Mountain Lake. I felt as if I were getting close to something. I next looked up anything to do with water. The references were both literal and figurative. I found Jesus being the water of life, the parting of the red sea, Noah's flood, and God creating water in the book of Genesis. Nothing set off my radar. Eventually I came to Psalm twenty-three and paused at another verse about water. This Psalm held a special place for our family. The farm got its name from verse one, but it was verse three that struck a chord.

I read aloud. "He maketh me to lie down in green pastures: he leadeth me beside the still waters."

Smith Mountain Lake wasn't still water, but my last thought before resurfacing at Smith Mountain Lake was of The Dismal Swamp. The swamp was a form of still water. I mentally recreated the walk around on Jeb Lawson's property. I recalled the approach from the driveway, the side porch, and layout of the cabin seen from the porch window. The small backyard and small shed with a battery bank for the solar. The lawn in front of the cabin was kind of like a green pasture. What would I see were I to lie down on that green pasture that sloped down to the still waters?

From the front lawn, I recalled the view of the dock, boat, and the road across the small inlet where I parked the Jeep. In my mind's eye I scanned back and forth. Off to the left were trees and the driveway which led up to the cabin, but to the right were woods and bushes and also a septic system vent pipe. Not an uncommon occurrence for properties off the beaten path who were not on town sewer. A fuzzy conversation from the Southfork Police Station came back to me.

"I cannot believe I missed this," I said, closing the Bible.

"What did you miss?" Annie said coming out to join me on the deck.

I dialed Tollers. While it rang, I turned to Annie. "Another long shot."

Tollers picked up. "Hey Brandon-"

I spoke without saying hello. "What did the cop say was in those two rooms at the cabin in the swamp?"

"Uhm a bedroom and bathroom," he said. "I think the bedroom had two twin beds and-"

"No," I almost yelled. "What was in the bathroom?"

"A toilet. Why?"

"What kind of toilet?"

"A compost toilet."

"Compost toilets don't need water, right?"

"Right. Just a vent pipe. You toss sawdust or something in it. I'm thinking of putting one in my RV and taking out my blackwater tank so I can boondock for longer periods of time and-"

I hung the phone up on my friend.

Annie slapped my shoulder. "That was so rude. He drove all the way out there with you-"

"Shush."

"Did you just shush me?"

Annie slapped my shoulder again. I, in turn, slapped my forehead. I remembered there was no sewer line going in, or out, from under the house. Only an electric line and the well line to the kitchen sink, which had an old lever pump for water which dumped excess back onto the ground under the cabin.

"I can't believe I missed this?"

"Missed what?"

"Hold on."

I dialed Bud, an associate from church, who was a retired plumber and septic technician.

He picked up. "Hello?"

"Bud, don't talk, just listen. Most septic systems need a vent, right?"

"Uh, sure."

"What are those septic systems you use for properties with high water tables, or where the leach fields fail?"

"Not really an issue in Halifax County, but there are options you can do to make a property usable."

"Such as?"

"A tight tank."

"Yes, a tight tank!" I said. "It's basically a self-contained holding tank that you have pumped, right?"

"Right. Normally a septic tank will have an outflow into a leach field. If kept in good condition you may never have to pump the system. With a tight tank it has no outflow. It's simply a huge porta potty that needs to be pumped when full."

"So it's waterproof?"

"Yeah, it's meant to sit at, or even below, a water table. Why?"

"Do you know if you could ever modify one of those watertight tanks?"

"In what way?"

"To use like one of those tornado shelters you see buried in people's backyards?"

"Sure, but the units I installed held poop instead of people. Only thing you'd need is good air flow."

"Air flow," I repeated, realizing the vent pipe in the yard wasn't simply off to the side but might have been hidden off to the side.

"What's this for?"

"It's for a case I'm working on. I have a weird theory. You'd think I'm crazy if I told you. Thanks."

"Call anytime."

I texted Drake to call me.

Annie sat in the rocking chair next to me. She seemed hesitant to press me. Finally, she said, "What's going on in your head?"

I fell back in the rocking chair and looked straight ahead. Cows were scattered in random patterns around the pasture. In the distance I could see our main pond with the two figures of Moss and Minnie. The sun reflected off its glass-like surface. Although the water was calm, I knew it was all a facade. A lot was going on just under the surface. Bugs were feeding on algae and fish were feeding on the bugs. Death and life were battling.

"Brandon?"

"I think Brooke could still be on that property?" I said.

"What? You guys searched it top to bottom?"

"What if she's in the swamp?"

"Huh?"

"Underwater."

"Like an underwater holding tank?" I nodded. "Brandon, we're in rural southern Virginia and you're talking about a scenario from a James Bond movie."

"Lawson has a vent pipe bringing oxygen somewhere. I initially thought it was for a septic system, but he doesn't have one, so that pipe is either for a condemned septic system, or it's providing air somewhere."

"And you think it's providing air to," she paused, "an underwater holding tank? Why underwater and not buried in the yard?"

"I would have seen some anomaly in the contour of the sloping yard, or a hatch somewhere. The vented pipe was hidden in the brambles just off the side of the lawn and surrounded by mature trees. There's no way a tank could be buried there and not disturb the decades-old trees."

"It just sounds crazy."

"I know, but the fact I'm pretty sure this Lawson guy

swapped messages with Annie's uncle over a pic of Brooke he shared. If Lawson is the guy who goes by the codename Beelzebub, then he asked for more pics of Brooke via messaging. This definitely makes him a suspect."

"But you said he lives in a beat-up cabin in the middle of the swamp. How does he have the money to build something like this?"

"Lawson had an expensive lawyer show up within minutes of being arrested. After speaking with Senator Schilling, I believe the lawyers were funded by Gaspar Schultz, which means Jeb Lawson is somehow affiliated with that sicko and has access to vast amounts of funds and resources."

Annie exhaled. "I'll admit, it is strange."

"Each fact on its own is thin, but the sum of the parts together…" I paused. "You know I-"

"Don't believe in coincidences," Annie said. "What are you gonna do?"

"I gotta go back for one more look."

"But what about the restraining order?"

"He doesn't own the water. Legally, I should be okay if I park across the way and swim over from opposite riverbank."

"Promise me you'll take someone with you?"

"I'm waiting to hear back from Drake. Don't say anything to Sally or JT. I can't give them false hope. This could all be for naught."

FOURTEEN

DRAKE STILL HADN'T CALLED ME BACK AND I WAS LEFT waiting with nervous energy. After placing an order for off-road diesel for the tractors, I drove out to the wooded portion of the property to shoot. I'd set up some cast iron pans for target practice. I used my Smith and Wesson but also fired some rounds from a Remington twelve gauge. The rhythmic shooting was a nice way to get my mind refocused. I hit near dead center at ten and fifteen yards with the handgun, but beyond that I needed improvement.

My cell rang as I pulled back into the barn with the UTV. It was an annoying default tone I needed to change. "This is Brandon?"

"Brandon, sorry for not getting back to you sooner," Drake said. "What's up?"

"I need to get back on Jeb Lawson's property."

"What do you need to look for?"

"I think Brooke's there."

"You said you searched the entire property and police searched the interior of the cabin from top to bottom and found nothing."

"What if I told you I thought she was being kept in a hidden holding tank."

"Where?"

I paused before saying, "Underwater?"

"Seriously?"

"It's possible with a custom self-contained unit like a tornado shelter."

"The guy's a poor hillbilly."

"I think it's all a facade. Gaspar Schultz is financing his lawyer. Clearly he has means."

"But how?"

"I think you could have a tight tank dropped in that swamp with ballasts and no one would know."

"You think a judge will issue a warrant based on that tin-foil-hat theory?"

"No, but thought I'd run it by you. You did say his brother lived in Elizabeth City, right?"

"Yeah, why?"

"Think about it. The Dismal Swamp Canal goes from Virginia down to Elizabeth City. He could reach his brother's property via boat. From there you can sail right into Albemarle Sound and eventually past the outer banks out to open water. It's a low-profile route if you were smuggling anything, be it drugs, or humans."

"Still a stretch to get a warrant," he said. "What are you gonna do?"

I paused. "I have to sneak back onsite to see for myself."

"You sure about this?"

"Yes."

Drake huffed. "I can't protect you. You're on your own if you go back there."

"I know, and I have a restraining order from when I was there last."

"Not the best time to go to jail when your wife's about to give birth."

I knew he wasn't trying to talk me out of going, just giving me a clear picture of what I was up against. The thought of not being there for the birth of my child was a gut-punch.

"When are you thinking of going back?" Drake said.

"After I get off the phone with you."

"You're sure about this?" he repeated.

The entire scenario at Smith Mountain Lake replayed in my mind in a fast forward picture. "Just say a prayer, brother."

In my bedroom closet was an old wooden sea chest that had been in my family for generations. On top rested wool sweaters and winter clothes I had recently put away for the season. I removed the coverings and opened the lid. Inside were several more handguns, extra ammo and mags, along with an AR-15 rifle mounted on the underside of the lid. They were all new purchases after I had a run-in with a domestic terrorist group. I almost purchased night vision goggles and a Kevlar vest to go with everything, but Annie claimed I was going all doomsday-prepper on her, so I settled on a night vision scope for the AR. I pulled the rifle and four thirty-round mags and loaded them into the Jeep. I came back in the house and grabbed a high-end flashlight and four additional mags for my Smith and Wesson along with a MOLLE vest. When I turned around, Annie stood in the closet entrance holding her belly like a weapon of guilt.

"Why are you taking all this gear?"

"I may need it based on my last encounter."

"Is Drake going with you?"

"He can't go."

"Tollers?"

"He could lose his job if he were to come with me again."

"Colt?"

"Still on his honeymoon."

"Then call the local PD."

"For what? This is just a theory I have. It could take them weeks to get the proper paperwork to get a warrant and it's doubtful a judge would issue one based on a crazed theory about a hidden underwater prison cell."

"Then maybe you should wait until—"

"Annie, what would you say if this were Emily? Would you tell me to wait or go?"

Annie broke eye contact. "What if you're wrong?"

"What if I'm right?"

She waved her hand like she was shooing an annoying fly. "Just go."

I leaned in to kiss her and she pushed me away. "If I kiss you, I'm afraid… Just go."

I paused, trying to think of words of comfort, but I couldn't guarantee my safe return and to say so would be lying. "I love you always," I said, walking past her.

It was almost eight p.m. when I pulled onto the dirt road that led to Jeb Lawson's cabin. I shut my lights off and drove by moonlight and memory. I took the left fork in the road and drove until the dirt trail turned to brush again. Parked in front of me was a blacked-out SUV with a DC license plate. I shut the Jeep off and walked around the vehicle, confirming no one was inside. The air was cool and there were very little noises. It was as if nature had been forewarned trouble was here.

"You can come out," I said in a low voice.

There was a crunch of leaves and a few snapped twigs. The next moment, Drake emerged from the bushes zipping up his fly.

"At my age, when nature calls you can't ignore it." My elderly African American friend was dressed in tactical khakis, boots, and some sort of hybrid black mock turtleneck. "Dang mosquitos are eating me alive," he said, waving his hand back and forth in front of his face.

"Is there a reason you're here?" I said.

"I knew you weren't going to listen to me, and I feel like it's my job to keep you out of trouble. Besides, I was in Norfolk when you called."

I knew he was putting his career on the line. "It could be nothing," I said.

"Probably is," he said, "so let's go recon and then go get some food. I'm hungry."

I wanted to hug the man in front of me. As far as friends went, I was deeply blessed. I opened the back of the Jeep and dropped a duffle bag onto the ground.

Drake pointed to the AR resting in the back. "What're you preparing for, zombies?"

"Sorry, it's the only thing I have with night vision."

Drake walked over to his SUV and opened the trunk. The interior lights in the modified vehicle were red for nighttime use. He unzipped his own duffle bag and removed two pairs of night vision goggles. "Here," he said handing me a pair of night vision goggles. "Leave the rifle and take these instead."

It took me a minute to remember how to adjust the goggles correctly. I hadn't worn them since my time in the Marines. They brought back memories, both fun and terrifying. I looked over at Drake who had his on. He gave me the thumbs up and we headed off down the road.

A muskrat, or some varmint, ran across our path and jumped into the water with a plop. The swamp's residents were now chirping, croaking, and making a racket. We could have spoken out loud and it would have been masked through all the chatter. We reached a clearing and stopped. About a hundred yards of water separated us from the beginning of the cabin's property. The area with the boat and dock were camouflaged by brush and a massive cypress tree. From the far shore the lawn climbed a hill about thirty-five yards up to Jeb's cabin. Lights were on and a shadow moved back and forth in the single window.

"What now?" Drake said. I dropped my bag onto the ground and pulled out a thin two-millimeter wetsuit, mask, and fins. "Are you crazy?" he said, pointing to the black water. "You're gonna go swim in that?"

I took off the night vision goggles and started to undress down to my underwear. "The only way I'm gonna confirm my theory is if I get over there and swim around. If I find nothing then we skedaddle, and no one ever knows we were here."

"You're braver than I thought."

"Actually, this water's not as bad as you think. The decaying spruce and juniper somehow keep the bacteria level down. Old sailing ships used to take the water from Lake Drummond with them for long voyages because it would last so long."

"Not what I meant. There's gonna be snakes and gators in there."

I spit in the mask to keep it from fogging up. "Doubtful we'd find gators this far north, though there have been rumors. Snakes are a real possibility though. That's why I'm wearing a hood and gloves."

Drake shuddered. "You get into trouble I ain't coming in after you. I don't like the water."

I put on a weight belt to give me neutral buoyancy and reached back into the bag for a small pony bottle of spare air, a waterproof flashlight, and dive knife which I strapped to the inside of my leg. I tip-toed into the shallows and sat down to put the fins on. The cool water entered the wetsuit and within moments it was heated by my body to a comfortable temperature. I gave the thumbs up and submerged.

Visibility was nonexistent and I kept the flashlight off unless necessary. I stayed a few feet below the surface so as to not attract attention with the bubbles. If I conserved air, I'd still only have a few minutes with the small tank of spare air. I kept my hands in front in case I ran into any submerged logs or critters. A few things moved off to my right I hoped were just fish. I reached the far side and surfaced under the rickety boat dock. Behind me, on the other side of the dock, was the boat. In front of me were reeds extending above the water.

From somewhere beyond the water came a muffled noise. Through the wetsuit hood, I couldn't locate or identify the sound. My stomach tightened when the sound turned out to be footsteps approaching. I remained still under the dock with only my head above water. The heavy steps came closer and stepped onto the dock. Their weight made the old boards creak. Whoever it was sounded like they were going to break through and land in the water next to me. It had to be Jeb Lawson.

He got to the end of the dock and started to relieve himself into the water off to the right. The flow of urine splashed back against my mask, but I couldn't move for fear of giving away my location.

"Take that," he grumbled.

A moment later an empty bottle of Jack Daniels plopped into the water in front of me. The bottle filled with water and disappeared. He grumbled a few more incoherent words in a slurred voice before walking back the way he had come.

A minute later, a screen door slammed up at the cabin. With the bottle of spare air in my mouth, I dropped under-water and pushed off the muddy bottom, swimming out from under the dock. A forearm size fish swam by which almost made me surface. I swam out into the channel and then stopped and turned to face the direction of dock and shore.

To the left was a natural peninsula which created a small semi-circular beach with the boat and dock on the opposite end of the curve. The muddy bottom was full of reeds. If there were anything hidden underwater it would not be in the channel but closer to shore inside this semi-circle. Starting near the peninsula, I worked my way back towards the direction of the dock. I stayed along the bottom feeling with my hands as it was too risky to turn the flashlight on. I was using a lot of air and my time would be limited. The mud gave way to sand and reeds, but visibility was still nonexistent. A moment later I bumped into something hard. I felt around and couldn't tell what I was against. I risked turning on the flashlight for a moment and faced a greenish wall of muck. I wiped the grime away and noticed a dark brown surface. I took a glove off and felt.

It was man-made.

FIFTEEN

It was difficult to tell how big the object was. I surfaced in the middle of a swath of reeds in chest-high water. I felt around and found the top of the object, above the water's surface. It was a circular camouflaged piece of metal. This portion that rose above the water was covered in vegetation, but the reeds attached to it were fake and meant to look like their real counterparts growing all around me. Recessed into the metal top was a wheel like you would find on a submarine door. I turned in Drake's direction and waved my arms back and forth to signify that I had found something.

I tried to turn the wheel on top. It spun but a moment later stopped with a clink. I risked turning the flashlight on for a moment. There was a padlock attached to the wheel. The only tool I had on me was the dive knife. I tried to pry the lock open with it, but it did nothing more than bend the blade. It took every ounce of discipline to leave the tank and swim back towards Drake's side of the swamp. I ran out of air halfway back and resurfaced, not caring about noise at this point.

"Drake, I found it," I said, throwing the empty air canister on the shore.

Drake had his goggles off, but I could see his eyes widen. "Lord have mercy. I'm gonna call this in."

"Do what you want," I said taking off the fins, "but I'm going back over there."

"We don't have a warrant or—"

"There's no way I'm waiting."

Drake was texting something. "Oh no," he said.

"What?"

"Cell signal's jammed."

"Forgot to tell you there's no signal out here. It's a dead zone."

He shook his head. "My cell's military grade. We got our own satellites. I should be getting a signal regardless." He looked skyward as if he could see the satellites orbiting the planet. "It's being jammed."

This reinforced my sense of urgency. "You better head back toward the street to get a signal and call for help."

"I ain't leaving you." He paused for a moment as if he realized we did need backup. "Is your jeep unlocked?"

"Yeah."

"I'll make a call and be back before you know it."

"I'd hurry if I were you."

"Why's that?"

"It's padlocked and I don't have any tools with me beyond a multi-tool in my vest, so the only way that tank's gonna be opened is with my gun."

"You just wait for me you hear," he whispered.

I placed my vest, which held my gun and spare mags, into the waterproof bag and started to swim back across the water pushing the waterproof floating bag in front of me. I reached the submerged tank and swam around it to the shore. On shore I swapped my mask, hood, gloves, and fins out for the vest. I waded back out to the reeds, found the hatch and aimed my pistol at the padlock. In a few seconds my world would change. Either I would discover a dark secret and attract a crazed hillbilly who would come out with guns blazing, or I would find nothing and attract a crazed hillbilly who would come out with guns blazing. Either way I was headed towards a firefight, and jail if I guessed wrong.

Logic drove the fears out of my mind. There was no other reason to have a hidden underwater tank surrounded by fake reeds unless you using it to smuggle something illegal whether it be humans, guns, or drugs. I remembered the air vent in the yard. It had to be what I thought it was. Military training kicked in as if to remind me that I should wait for Drake to return. He should be positioned between me and the cabin to watch my six, but I only saw a timer in my mind. An image of Brooke Eldridge was replaced by my daughter's face. A moment later Emily's face morphed into a picture of my infant son, Jonah.

I looked skyward and whispered, "I trust you, Lord."

I tightened my grip on the pistol and fired off a single round. The nine-millimeter sounded like a cannon as the padlock exploded in front of me. A timer went off in my mind. I guessed that it would take fifteen-seconds for someone to get from the cabin to me. I didn't care. I had to see what was inside.

I flicked what was left of the smoking lock into the water and spun the wheel as fast as I could with my free hand. In the distance a door crashed open. A few seconds later a gun went off from somewhere near the cabin. There was a crash and more gunfire, but this gun was not as loud, revealing there were two guns and two shooters. Something splashed near me and a bullet hit the tank with a clinking noise. I spun the wheel some more and a moment later it stopped. A whoosh of air escaped as I lifted the heavy metal lid. What smelled like human waste overpowered my nostrils. Maybe it was just a septic tight tank and I was a fool? I gagged and forced the flashlight into the hole. Water dripped into the tank from around the lid. A ladder descended at least eight feet to the bottom of the tank. It was dry and appeared to veer off in both a left and right direction. Something slithered away from the beam of light. Was it an animal, a snake, or a human leg? I couldn't tell.

"Anyone in there?" I shouted into the tank.

The only response I received was splashes as semi-automatic gunfire peppered the water around me. I dropped behind the lid of the tank back into the water. I fired back in the direction of the cabin. My gunshot was like a homing beacon as more rounds splashed closer to me with some hitting the tank with a clang. Why had I rushed into the scenario? I should have waited for Drake. There was splashing on the other side of the tank. It was in the water and was a person running towards me from the shallows. I waited with my gun facing the direction. A moment later, Drake jumped from the boat onto the dock and down into the water next to me holding my AR above his head.

"I should have never gotten in the water," he said, lifting the goggles up.

Bullets hit the tank and I pulled Drake behind the tank with me. "Keep your head down."

"So, what's the plan now that we're both going to jail."

"Did you get a message out?"

He shook his head. "I heard gunfire, grabbed your rifle and ran down the driveway to get here." He pointed to the water. "Cell's in my pants pocket and it's toast. We're on our own."

I reached over the top of the tank and fired off the remaining rounds in my magazine. I dropped the mag into the water and fell back behind the tank to reload.

"We've gotta fall back to a better position," Drake said. "We're gonna be like shooting fish in a barrel here. We're underpowered and tactically disadvantaged."

I tapped the tank with my gun. "We can't leave. I think there's someone in there."

"If we get killed, we're no use to anyone. They can flank us through the woods and come up there," he said, pointing to my left where the small peninsula was.

"I'm not leaving," I said.

"I've followed you this far. Now it's time you listen to me, Son."

I reluctantly nodded. "Okay. Call it."

"We have to move. Either back the way I came or straight ahead."

It had been such a long journey to get to this point. I didn't want to leave, but knew he was right. "Roger that," I said, moving off to the left towards shore. "Stay here. I'll be the decoy."

"Brandon, you knucklehead. Get back here."

I ran through the shallow water towards the small peninsula. This was the ideal direction they could flank us from. I made it to shore and ran through briars and saplings like a baby elephant walking on balloons. More gunfire came from the cabin towards the tank. It was clear there were two men with guns firing from the porch. I ran off to the left where the foliage was thicker crashing through more bushes and saplings. Gunfire hit the area I had just stepped. Suddenly, lights went off all around me. I looked up and found solar powered motion lights spread over various tree branches. A redneck make-shift early warning system. I ducked behind a large tree.

There was a lull in gunfire. "I know you're there," Jeb Lawson's voice shouted with the thick drawl I remember. "You've been warned before." His voice was close. "This here's self-defense. You ain't leaving this property alive, Mr. Brandon Hall from Nathalie Virginia."

The stupid floodlights were gonna be the death of me. I shot the two closest out but didn't risk trying for the others as I needed to conserve ammo. A shot ripped through the tree I hid behind. It was more than likely a bolt action deer rifle.

"Hold yer fire, Jeb. You almost hit me."

Another round hit the back of the tree. This time I was sure it was an AR. "Around the side," one of them said.

Branches and twigs snapped to my left. I couldn't back-track to the water as it was too far, and I'd be cut down in the process. I popped my head around the left side of the tree and quickly moved to the right. The bark on the left exploded. I reached around the right side and fired off the remaining six rounds from my clip. The first two rounds went wild, but I locked in on Jeb and hit him at least twice in the chest. He fell back, dropping his deer rifle. A moment later he sat up revealing a plated vest. He leveled a 1911 pistol and started unloading in my direction. I ducked behind the tree again and dropped the mag to reload. To the left, more floodlights went off as Joss broke through the woods. These guys were fearless, or simply too dumb to care.

From the direction of the house, the sound of an AR-15 went off. I could tell it was my rifle. Drake had flanked them. Both men started firing indiscriminately. Nothing happened around me which meant they were aiming back towards the cabin. I poked my head around the tree. Joss had moved back towards the property line outside the flooded light. I did not have a clear shot, but I could see he was reloading his rifle while Jeb continued to fire his pistol in front of me somewhere. I pulled the flashlight from my vest and pressed it three times in succession to put it into flashing mode. It was now like a solar flare in the forest.

I shouted back towards the cabin and Drake. "Painting target."

I threw the flashlight in the direction of Joss. By some miracle it didn't hit any tree branches and landed behind him. From what I could tell he didn't seem to care about a flashing light. The sound of the AR went off, and a moment later Joss fell back flat on the ground. Unlike Jeb, he didn't get back up. Even if he were wearing a heavy-duty plated vest, the AR hit would keep him down for a minute.

"Joss, you Okay?" Jeb shouted. "Joss?"

A moment later I heard the sound of breaking branches. I crept back around the other side of the tree to try to locate Jeb, but he was gone.

"You okay?" Drake shouted from somewhere near the cabin.

"I'm good," I said. "I lost Jeb. Heads up, he could be coming towards you."

"Negative. I'd have eyes on him if he were."

I turned back towards Joss' direction. He was still down next to the blinking flashlight. I kept my pistol on him and moved through the thickets. I fired off a round into the mud next to his head to see if he was playing possum. He didn't move. When I reached him I knew why. A round from the AR had caught him in the head.

"Joss is down," I said.

A rumble came from the water where the boat was. I rushed back through the trees the way I came.

"Brandon?" Drake shouted.

"It's Jeb," I shouted back. "He's on the boat. Get back to the tank."

Instead of heading back towards the boat dock I went through thick brush towards the small peninsula. I knew Jeb would pass by with the boat to get out into open water. If Jeb got away, he could virtually disappear into the vast swamp. I broke through the thickets and had about five feet of clear dirt before it dropped off into the water. I stopped and waited in a crouched position. Jeb throttled the boat. It was off the dock and heading towards me. He was crouched down low in a smart tactical position behind the console of the boat. I didn't try for him as he was too hard of a target wearing the plated vest. Instead, as the boat passed by, I unloaded several rounds into the outboard engine. The pinging noise was followed by smoke and a moment later the engine stalled and the boat slowed down.

I reloaded and stepped into the shallows waiting for what I knew would happen. The shadowy figure of Jeb rose up from behind the seat and started firing off rounds from his pistol in my direction. His shots veered left and high. He didn't have a bead on me, but I did on him. However, because of his vest I had to make it a head shot. It was a twenty-yard bullseye on a moving target in almost pitch dark. I fired a shot and missed. I fired again and missed again. He dove overboard with a splash. I didn't see him resurface. The momentary lull in gunfire left the swamp in complete silence. It was unnerving

Beyond the boat on the far bank I could see movement. I fired off three rounds blindly in the direction thinking it was Jeb climbing out of the swamp. Without daylight it was a wasted effort. There was a shout from somewhere behind me.

I yelled back to Drake. "You okay?"

"I'm at the tank. I need you."

I ran into the shallows back towards the tank. Drake's torso stuck out from the top of the tank. He shined a flashlight in my direction momentarily blinding me.

"What did you find?"

He shook his head back and forth. "Not good."

"Children?"

"Two."

"Is one of them Brooke?" I pleaded.

"Yes."

"Please tell me she's alive?"

"Barely," he said, but he seemed unhappy.

"That's great news." Images of JT and Sally smiles flooded my mind.

"There's another child," he said. "A young boy. From what I can tell he's recently deceased."

Images assaulted my mind of Annie's car accident and my son's lifeless body. I stopped at the tank.

"Brandon, this tank is punctured from the gunfire. Water's leaking in like a sieve. I need you to come down inside with me."

"I can't."

"What do you mean?"

"I can't," I wheezed, almost hyperventilating.

"I need you, Brandon."

The only words I could get out were, "Jonah-"

"Your friend's child is down there. She's alive. I need your help to get her out."

I was a coward. I gritted my teeth and grumbled to myself, "Man-up."

"Brandon?"

I motioned with my hand for Drake to go back inside the tank. I climbed inside as my friend rushed to the bottom and moved out of sight. The smell was horrific. I realized it wasn't just human waste, but human decomposition. I stopped long enough to vomit into the darkness not caring if my bile mixed in with the toxic recipe below. I reached the bottom and could almost stand up without hitting my head. Drake stood behind me, blocking the view. Water dripped all around us. He pointed beyond me with his flashlight. In the shadowy light was a dirty little girl holding onto a dirtier teddy bear. She was curled up with dark water pooling around a blanket she rested upon. Her eyes were wide like a rabid animal with terror imprinted on them.

"Brooke, do you remember me? It's Mr. Hall from church." She didn't acknowledge me. "My daughter is Emily. She helps out in your Sunday school class?" Still nothing. I reached out my hand. "Do you want me to take you out of here?" She nodded back and forth; a clear no. I pointed to the ankle-high water. "It's getting wet in here and I need to get you back to your momma. Would you like that?"

She thought about it for a moment and surprised me with the word, "Yes."

I didn't touch her but instead held my hand in a fixed position near her. She needed to come to me, or else I might be perceived as a threat. She reached out a shaking hand and placed it in mine. I didn't close my hand but lifted it up and she rose. I motioned with my free hand to come to me. She did, and a moment later the embrace she gave me was like a vice. I placed the teddy bear on the blanket, but she started to whimper. She stopped when I handed it back to her. The teddy bear smelled like urine and filth.

"Can you carry her up the tunnel?" Drake said.

"I got her," I said. "What about—"

"I'll take care of him."

Before starting up the ladder I saw the dim shape of a shadowed small body lying behind Drake. I realized my friend stood in the way so I wouldn't have to see the boy. The smell was horrific. It took every ounce of self-control not to vomit again.

"Please God," I said, climbing the ladder. "Please don't leave us."

SIXTEEN

I crested the entry hatch and realized we had left it completely unguarded. I knew Jeb was on the run, but if he had doubled-back he could have locked us all in the tank to drown. It was a dumb mistake made in a blind rush to help the child. Fortunately, Jeb was nowhere in sight. Stepping out of the hatch and into the water was difficult holding Brooke, but I wasn't about to let her go. We splashed down on the shore-side of the tank in waist-high water and she started to cry.

"It's okay, darlin," I whispered. "I got you."

I could hear the echo of Drake splashing around in the tank. I couldn't imagine the horror he was dealing with.

I got to shore and headed towards the cabin with Brooke cradled in my arms. I snuck my gun out from the shoulder holster without alerting her. Off to the left in the woods, my flashlight still flickered like an otherworldly beacon. Lying next to it was the dark outline of Jeb's dead brother. I was happy Drake had taken that shot rather than me.

Once I was on the cabin porch, I stopped in front of the window. I turned the child away and did a quick scan. No one else was inside. The entry door was wide open. I scanned the room a second time before stepping inside. Still holding Brooke, I checked the bedrooms and bathroom which were both clear as well. On a table was a shortwave radio, but no landlines or cell phones. Two laptops in the bedroom had been shot up. A clear sign Jeb and his brother were trying to destroy evidence of some kind.

I re-holstered my gun and placed Brooke down on the couch. I had to pry her hands from around my neck. Like an elastic band they snapped back over her soggy teddy bear. I used my pen light to check her pupil dilation. She wasn't in shock but a close runner up. I draped a quilted blanket around her.

Drake entered and lowered the AR when he saw me. "Any sign of Jeb?" he said, handing me the rifle.

"Negative," I said, taking up guard at the door. "He took off after I shot out his boat. He made it to the far shore, but I lost him."

"Let him go for now," Drake said, checking on Brooke without touching her. "How you doing, Sweetie?" She didn't respond. Drake adjusted the blanket draped around her. "Let me see if I can find a cartoon on the television."

While he did that, I scanned the property back and forth using the night vision scope on the AR. There was no movement in the front yard all the way down to the water. A small still form lay on the wooden boat dock covered over with a blanket. It was the size of a small boy. On the far shore the boat was stuck in the muddy bank, still issuing a wisp of smoke from the engine. A minute later I heard a Bugs Bunny cartoon come on the flat screen television. Elmer Fudd talked about *hunting wabbits.*

Drake came back to the open door. "My cell phone's junk," he said. I pointed to a short-wave radio on a coffee table near Brooke. "That's the only thing we got."

Drake sat in front of the short-wave radio messing with the dials. "Haven't used one of these since CIA training decades ago."

"Aha, so you're CIA?" I said, continuing to scan the property. "I knew it."

"Used to be," he chuckled. "Keep guessing." Drake snapped his fingers. "Jackpot."

"What?"

"They left a cell phone under a pile of papers." He checked it over and whistled. "And this baby's military grade." He dialed a number. "And it has a signal. Whatever jamming device they're using must be focused from the cabin outward, or the cabin has a booster of some kind." Seconds later he was connected to someone. "This is zulu, tango, four, two, one, five. I got a situation at Dismal Edge Drive in Southfork. Lock on to this phone's signal. I'll need LEO on site along with an EMT. Send any Homeland, ATF, and FBI in the area as well." There was a pause and Drake added, "Be advised when sending help; we're in the wilderness. Four-wheel drive vehicles might be needed."

After he hung up, I said, "Make sure you activate the GPS location on the cell."

He waved his hand and huffed. "Doesn't matter. They'll activate it and track us here."

The government's ability to climb into our lives never ceased to amaze me. Drake came back to the door and took the AR from me to resume guard duty. "You better notify the girl's momma."

I used the same cell phone to dial JT's number. He picked up on the first ring. "Hello?"

"It's Brandon-"

"What number are you calling from?"

"Long story. Is Sally with you?"

He put it on speaker phone. "She's right next to me."

"I have Brooke," I said. "She's safe."

There was a scream in the background from Sally. When JT finally stopped praising God, the one word he said was, "Where?"

"Same place we checked in the Dismal Swamp. There was an underwater holding tank that I missed."

"An underwater what?"

"Long story."

"What made you think to go back."

"You could say I had a message from God."

Sally took the phone and spoke through weeping. "Oh Brandon, I don't know how to thank you."

"I'm going to try to video conference you guys in, but the signal may or may not work. Just know Brooke's still borderline in shock."

I changed the phone to video mode and knelt down next to Brooke. On the television, Elmer Fudd was having a hard time catching that *wascally wabbit*. "Brooke, do you want to see your mommy?" Brooke didn't respond. "I'm going to show you your mom, okay?"

She nodded and I turned the phone to face her. Sally was showing a tremendous amount of strength keeping her emotions in check. "Hi, Brooke, baby. I'm walking out to the car right this very second, and we're coming to get you okay?"

Brooke didn't respond. Sally started to talk about how much she missed Brooke and that they were going to get her that puppy she always wanted when they got her home. Sally said she would never let her out of their sight again and kept apologizing like it was her fault. Holding the phone in front of Brooke, I saw nothing in the young girl's eyes. She was alive and breathing, but her eyes had no life in them. The spark had been wiped out from shock, terror, or some other evil act she'd experienced. Sally had a long road ahead of her with Brooke's recovery. I wanted to kill Jeb Lawson. I had never wanted to kill a man this much in my entire life. This included the drunk driver who took my son's life. What that man did was wrong, but it was unintentional. What Jeb and his brother did was pure, unadulterated, premeditated evil.

A conservation officer was the first on site. Drake met him outside and must have shown him some form of ID because when they entered into the cabin the officer kept calling him sir. Five minutes later more law enforcement officers showed up along with an EMT. I kept Sally on video conference the entire time so she could see what was happening. One of the techs went to pick Brooke up to place her on a gurney so they could bring her to the waiting ambulance. Brooke moved her hand in a rapid motion and latched on my arm.

"I'm guessing you're the one who found her?" The man said. I nodded. "You should be the one to carry her."

"Brandon, do what he says," Sally said. "Call us back when you can. Just promise me you won't leave her side."

"I promise," I said, hanging up the phone and placing it back on the table as it was now evidence.

Drake had retrieved my dive bag which I slung over my shoulder. The dirt road leading up to the cabin was now lit up with blue and red emergency lights flickering from grills and roofs of various marked, and unmarked, vehicles. Flashlights moved back and forth as law enforcement offi-cers ran up and down the driveway. Flares were staked into the ground along with chemical glow sticks to help light the way. Twice, a random officer tried to stop me when they saw my chest rig and gun. Each time Drake stepped in to my defense. By this time, Drake had two federal agents and a state trooper as part of his entourage.

I placed Brooke down on a gurney outside an ambulance and held her hand as they inspected her. The only noise she made was a quick cry when the teddy bear fell from her hand onto the ground. I lifted up the stuffed bear and placed it back in her arms. She grabbed it like a jealous child who never gave me permission to hold her toy.

One of the officer's wives ran a clinic in Southfork which they opened up as a staging area until Sally arrived. I drove in the ambulance with Brooke who held my hand the entire time. At the clinic, two off-duty doctors came in to give Brooke the initial exam and set her up with an IV as she was dehydrated. Police brought in food and put a Veggie Tales cartoon on television while we waited for Sally to show up. The entire time Brooke wouldn't let go of my hand

"What's the protocol?" I whispered to a nearby FBI agent who had just shown up.

"She's stable, we wait for the mom then we'll transport the girl and mom back to Halifax Regional Hospital where they can keep her for a day or two to run tests and observe her." The agent leaned into me. "You're either a genius or some freak of nature to have figured this out."

"I'm no genius," I said.

"Then what made you think to look in the swamp?"

"Would you believe me if I said divine intervention?"

He shook his head back and forth. "At this point, I would. I've never seen anything like this."

"What are the legal implications for me trespassing?"

The agent waved his hand. "Gonna be a lot of red tape,

but it's not like Jeb Lawson will be in any position to press charges. My agents are scouring that property. It looks like he was trafficking people through the canal via boat into North Carolina where waiting boats could then take the children out to open water, and any country in the world. What you uncovered is gonna have us rethinking how people are trafficked for years to come."

I turned back to Brooke tucked in the hospital bed wearing a clean, oversized hospital gown. She held onto me with one hand and her dirty stuffed animal with the other. All the while she stared at the television. I wasn't sure if she even saw the cartoon or was reliving a nightmare. The thought of Jeb Lawson on the loose made me furious. I wanted to be part of the manhunt to find him.

Drake brought my jeep over to the clinic along with a cup of coffee. "It's getting crowded around here," he said, pointing to the roomful of local, state, and federal agents. "It's time for me to vamoose. You need anything else?"

"Thanks for everything," I said. "You got a ride back to your vehicle?"

"One of the agents is taking me back," he said. "Call me in a few days to let me know how everything's going."

I shook his hand. "Thanks for everything."

"Today the good guys won, but tomorrow's a new day."

"And evil doesn't sleep," I added.

No sooner had Drake left when there was a commotion at the entrance of the clinic. JT burst through the door followed by Sally who rushed in and fell down at the foot of the bed. Sally looked like she had aged ten years since I last saw her. Brooke didn't turn from the cartoon.

"Oh, my baby!" Sally cried, taking Brooke's hand from me and raising it to her lips to kiss. "Oh, my sweet precious baby." Brooke still didn't reply.

A female doctor came over and placed her hand on Sally's shoulder. "You're going to need to give her time; she's been traumatized."

Sally turned to me, tears pouring down her face. "I don't care. I got my baby back. Brandon, I don't know how you did this-"

I held up my hand. "Once I explain, you'll realize I had nothing to do with it."

The room was stuffed to capacity and I started to shuffle through the crowd towards the door. I wanted nothing more than to get home to the farm and my girls. Between finding Brooke and the shootout, I was both physically, and emotionally, exhausted. Just as I reached the door someone grabbed my shoulder. I turned to see JT, tears streaming down his face.

"I don't know what to say."

I pulled on his arm, motioning him into the lobby. When we were outside the room I said, "Brooke's not the same girl she was. Give her time, okay?"

He nodded and started to say something but got choked up. He held up his hand as if to say to, *give me a minute.* Unable to collect himself, he simply hugged me before turning to walk back into the room.

I found a bathroom and changed from my wetsuit back into street clothes. When I exited, two FBI agents ushered me over to a table. The FBI had already set up a small headquarters in the front of the clinic, which was where I made statements and filled out paperwork for the next hour. Curtains were drawn to block out the media vehicles and cameras forming in the front parking lot. The agents interviewing me were shocked when I told them about my ordeal on Smith Mountain Lake and how I believed it led me to uncover Jeb Lawson's underwater holding cell. A few times they pressed me like I withheld some other piece of evidence. I was very sympathetic as the report they'd file was going to look like it was pulled from an episode of the X-Files television show. Coupled with the fact that a redneck private investigator solved this high-profile case would be a PR nightmare for the bureau. Before I got up to leave, they made me hand over my handgun as evidence. I was told that I'd maybe get it back.

A short while later I found myself out behind the clinic in a dark parking lot. The Jeep was parked next to a dumpster under dim light. I knelt down on the gravel, giving thanks for the message that God beat into my thick skull. A few minutes later I tore out of the parking lot via a back dirt road to avoid the media out in front of the clinic. On the way out of town I found the same gas station I had visited when I first entered Southfork. Inside, the same kid with the mullet was behind the counter. I found the biggest cup of coffee they sold and approached the counter. He looked at me in an odd way.

"Long time no see," I said.

"A lot of crazy things have happened since you showed up looking at that land."

"Odd coincidence," I said, handing him two bucks and walking away.

Before I exited the store, he said, "I don't believe in coincidences."

I turned and winked. "Neither do I."

Back in the Jeep I chugged half the coffee and could feel my energy increase like a battery being recharged. It was a temporary kick but would be enough to get me back to the farm. The entire drive home my phone kept ringing. I assumed most of the calls were law enforcement looking for more details. The only call I answered was from Annie.

"We got her," I said.

"I heard. I don't even know what to say."

"I had nothing to do with it," I said. "It was a God thing."

Outside the windshield I read signs for the city of South Boston with forty miles written under it. My farm was another twenty-five minutes beyond that. I couldn't wait to get home and crawl into bed.

"How do you feel?" Annie said.

"Exhausted. I'm looking forward to a good night's sleep. Why?"

"I uh, don't mean to add to your stress but you may not be able to go to bed right away."

"Why? What's wrong?"

"I think the baby's coming."

"Are you sure?" I said, hoping it was false labor pains.

"I'm sure. My water broke." I upended the rest of the coffee and shook the cup hoping to get the last drops out. "Hello, earth to Brandon?"

"I'm here," I said. "Are you okay to drive?"

"I think so."

"I'll meet you at the hospital. Remember, when you drive Hazel, she needs a few seconds to warm up. Third gear sometimes sticks too."

She giggled, "Nothing like a redneck birth in southern Virginia."

"Be safe, and I'll see you shortly. Love you." I hung up and looked out the windshield at the starlit night sky. We lived in one of the darkest spots on the eastern seaboard which made for great star gazing, but I looked beyond the stars. "Thank you," I said.

When I arrived at the hospital, Annie was checking in with Emily. I kissed them both and sat down next to Annie.

Emily sniffed me. "Daddy, you smell like-"

"Swamp? I know. I didn't get a chance to shower."

Annie rolled her eyes. "I drive myself to the hospital in

a forty-year-old-rust bucket. My husband shows up smelling like swamp water. This is not how people give birth on Hallmark movies of the week."

"First off, Hazel is not a rust bucket. And second we'll have a nice story to tell at John Wayne Hall's wedding about the night he was born."

Both my wife and daughter rolled their eyes.

A short while later, Annie was checked into a single room in the maternity ward. A nurse hooked her up to all sorts of high-tech monitors. Once the nurse said that everything looked good, I jumped into the small shower in the room's bathroom. It was nice to wash off the swamp water, but I had to put back on the same clothes which had absorbed some of the scent.

I came out of the bathroom smelling my armpits. "Well, I'm about seventy-five percent better."

"Nice of you to take a shower while your wife goes into labor."

My dad stood over Annie while Mom sat next to her in a wheelchair. I had forgotten they were still here. "Long story," I said leaning down to kiss my mom on her head. "How're you feeling?"

"Leaving first thing in the morning."

"Praise God."

Dad came over and shook my hand. "Brooke's rescue is all over the news. I'm proud of you, Brandon."

I pointed to the ceiling. "I had very little to do with it."

"Amen," my mom said.

Emily stood up against a floor to ceiling window looking out onto Route 501. "Daddy, somethings going on outside."

I walked over to the window. Below us, lights of various colors flashed from EMT's, police, sheriff, and local news vehicles. "I bet Sally and Brooke are on their way in."

Annie winced in pain. "Ouch, ouch, ouch. Brandon, go get the nurse."

I opened the door and faced Jamie, who was dressed in her hospital scrubs with a stethoscope slung around her neck. She looked more focused than normal.

She waved her hand side-to-side to let me know I was in her way. "Where's my patient?"

I held the door open and pointed towards Annie. She walked in and gave Mom a gentle hug before approaching the bed. Jamie picked up Annie's wrist and looked at her watch. "How're you feeling, Annie?"

"I'm in a lot of pain."

Jamie nodded. "Having a hard time catching your breath?" Annie nodded. Jamie snapped her fingers and pointed at me. "All males out. Emily sweetie, you should go into the hall as well. Grandma can stay if she'd like."

Dad, Emily, and me stepped into the hallway. A female nurse passed by to assist Jamie. Emily lifted her hands like she used to do when she was six years old. It was a motion for me to pick her up. My back tightened when I lifted her up as if to remind me my baby girl was no longer a little snuggle-bug.

About fifteen minutes later the nurse exited followed by Jamie who wheeled my mom's chair. "You can go see your wife now."

"How is she?"

"Fine, but I hope you're rested up. It could be a long night."

I was exhausted. The romantic idea I had of this birth was similar to Annie's made-for-television movie. I pictured us both well-rested and me dressed nice and smelling clean.

"Ultrasound was good," Jamie said. "Want to know the sex?"

"Yes," Emily shouted.

"We've waited this long," I said. "We can wait a bit longer.

"I've gotta go check on two other patients," Jamie said. "I'll be back in a little while. Have me paged if anything changes though. Oh, and Brandon-"

"Yes?"

"Nice job with Brooke."

I put Emily down next to my father. "Why don't you go up to your grandmother's room?"

"Good idea," my mother said. "They have reruns of The Rifleman on my TV."

Both Dad and Emily perked up when they heard this. I kissed my mom and daughter and told them I'd text Dad with updates. As the three of them waited by the elevator, I thought how nice it was that we were all here on this particular night. It was strange to think that Mom had been at the hospital for a life-threatening reason, while Annie was here for a life-giving reason, and somewhere else in the hospital Brooke was being looked over for a life-affirming reason. God was good and had been faithful to our three families. At that moment, the hospital felt like a blessed safe haven.

Back in the room, Annie's eyes were shut. I picked up her hand and kissed it lightly.

"Epidurals are a gift from God," she whispered.

"I thought you agreed to just bite down on a piece of leather and go without painkillers."

"Please shut up so I can sleep for a few minutes."

I laughed. Annie was funniest when she was stressed. The air conditioner was set on high as Annie was uncomfortable. With the baby in her belly, she was like a walking space heater. The leather chair next to her bed reclined into a small make-shift bed. I found a thin blanket and lay down across from her. My wife's face had no makeup on, and her hair was disheveled, but all I saw was the most beautiful woman in the world.

SEVENTEEN

What seemed like hours later, someone kicked my foot. I looked up to see Jamie standing over me with another female nurse. "Wake up, sleepy head."

Annie was awake. "You were snoring," she said. "You must be exhausted."

"Only you would worry about your husband during a time like this," Jamie said. "You're pathetic, Brandon."

"I know," I said, getting up. "And I like it that way."

One of the nurses gave me scrubs and a mask to place on over my clothes. For the next hour I held Annie's hand and prayed while Jamie worked behind a sheet at Annie's waist. I had participated in dozens of bovine births. Some went smooth, and others needed my assistance. I never worried much, but with Annie I felt helpless. I deferred completely to Jamie. If she needed me to stand on my head and cluck like a chicken, I was prepared to follow orders. Another nurse came in to assist. Another monitor was plugged in, and another ultrasound was done. I kept asking if everything was fine and kept being told to calm down by both Jamie and my wife.

Annie didn't yell during contractions but grunted really loud and gripped my hand tightly. At one point her nails drew blood from my wrist but I didn't care. She was a trooper. In between contractions my wife seemed to nod off to a half-sleep. During one of these moments I realized how fortunate we were to live in a day where modern medicine was available for births. Still, it was no walk in the park for women. My mind wandered back to the Garden of Eden. Man's punishment for disobeying God was that he would toil in the ground for the rest of his life to squeeze out a living. For women they were given a painful childbirth. From my point of view, woman seemed to have it worse.

A passage from John sixteen came to mind which explained how women suffer during childbirth, but after the child is born she remembers the pain no more. Embedded in the passage of painful childbirth was an image of us passing from this life into eternity. The pain and evil of this world will one day give way to joy and we will remember the pain no more. Even in our punishment, God has given us an escape hatch because of His Son.

A cry snapped me from the theological daydream. Not a woman's cry but the cry of a newborn baby.

Jamie's voice was softer now. "Want to cut the umbilical cord to your daughter?"

"My daughter?" I repeated. Annie's crying mixed in with the baby's. The beautiful baby in front of me was so tiny with pink skin. Her toothless wails were pitch perfect. Jamie handed me a pair of scissors. I cut through what felt like leather and the child was whisked away. Within minutes a swaddled clean baby was placed in Annie's waiting arms. My wife's crying turned to heavy sobs. I knew somewhere in the joy of her tears was the sad memory of holding our last child. Our Jonah.

"She's beautiful," I said, now crying as well.

"And look," Annie pointed to the blonde hair peeking out from a tiny pink cap on her head. "She's got a little peach fuzz already."

For the next half hour nurses came and went, cleaning up both Annie and the room. At this point a marching band could have come through and I don't think my wife would have cared. She just kept staring at the precious gift in her arms. I forced myself to turn away from the baby just long enough to text my dad, mom, and Emily pictures.

"Well, I guess John Wayne Hall's out of the question." I chuckled. "I guess she's gonna have to be May West Hall then?"

Annie looked down at the precious child. "Addison. Her name is Addison."

"Hi Addison," I said. "It's nice to meet you."

The rest of the night was a wonderful blur. I remember walking down the hall with my parents and Emily to see Addison in the infant ward. I remember eating a bagel and helping and orderly set up an extra cot in my mom's room so Emily and my dad could both stay there. I fell asleep in the chair across from Annie for a few hours but was woken when a nurse brought Addison in to feed in the early morning hours. I used the opportunity to wander out to my truck and find my emergency bag with spare clothes. When I turned to head back inside a bright light momentarily blinded me. A microphone was thrust in my face and a reporter started asking questions about Brooke Eldridge.

I asked them to move aside. When they didn't comply, I tried to walk around them, but another microphone and camera blocked my path. A familiar male voice I couldn't place said something about moving out of the way. I turned to see Tollers in his Sheriff's uniform pushing a cameraman back.

He motioned to me with his hand. "This way, Brandon."

I felt like a prize fighter being ushered from the crowd into the ring. I was so tired I couldn't even form the words to thank him. I patted my friend on the shoulder and re-entered the hospital. Tollers stayed to block the reporters while I found my way back to Annie's room. The baby was gone, and Annie had fallen asleep. I took another shower and changed into clothes that smelled like detergent rather than swamp water. I found the blanket and chair again and let my body shut down.

At some point Annie's sweet voice woke me. "Why don't you go home for a few hours?"

The sun peeked through a blind. "What time is it?" I said.

"Not sure. Somewhere around midday, I think. Addison will be back soon for another feeding."

I ran my hand through my beard and hair and waited as the room came into focus. The only words I could get out were, "coffee" and "back soon".

I put on my boots, kissed my wife and wandered out of the room. A nurse wheeled an infant past me, but I was so delirious I couldn't tell if it was my daughter or not. In the cafe I purchased a blueberry muffin and a large coffee and started to walk back. Normally I'd take the stairs, but this time I opted for the elevator. When the elevator doors opened, I saw JT who looked as tired as I felt.

"What are you doing here?"

"Baby arrived last night."

He perked up. "Seriously? Congratulations! Is it a boy or girl?"

"A healthy girl," I said. "How's Brooke?"

"She's dehydrated and malnourished, but alive and safe. I can't thank you enou-"

I held up my hand. "You'd have done it for me. Besides I

had very little to do with it." I proceeded to explain my revelation while Emily and I were underwater at Smith Mountain Lake. JT's jaw kept opening wider as the story got more fantastic.

"I guess you did have nothing to do with it," he said, lightly punching me in the shoulder. "We're getting discharged in an hour. Can you come up to see Sally and Brooke before we leave?"

Part of me didn't want to go. I was traumatized by the event and wanted to put it behind me. Selfishly, I was afraid it would taint the joyful birth of Addison, but I nevertheless agreed. JT led me up to a room with a state police officer posted outside to keep the media out. We entered a private room. Sally was resting in a chair next to Brooke who was asleep in bed. A few bags were packed and waiting by the door. Two gorgeous flowering plants were on the floor next to them. Brooke had been washed and looked healthier. A faint glow had returned to her pale skin. Looking at the sleeping child, I wondered if she was having good dreams or nightmares. Beside her in bed rested the stained teddy bear. Sally stirred and got up when she saw me. A moment later she had me in a bear hug of an embrace. Both of us started to cry.

She started to thank me again when I interrupted. "Let's have a moment of prayer." Everyone agreed. "Heavenly Father, I thank you for the miracles you provided which brought this child home. Please watch Brooke, and we pray for her full healing in Jesus' name." I looked over at JT and Sally. "And all the people said?"

"Amen."

As I went to leave, Brooke stirred. She looked around the room seeming confused as to where she was. Sally walked over and picked up her hand. "Guess who came to visit you?"

Brooke didn't say anything but just stared at me as if I were unrecognizable. A moment later a smile formed on her lips. I returned the smile and blew her a kiss before exiting. Back in Annie's room, Mom, Dad, and Emily were gushing over Addison. Mom was still in a wheelchair wearing a nice red dress.

"You going to a dance?" I said.

"I'm not leaving this hospital dressed in pajamas," Mom said. "That would be so undignified."

"Always the debutante," I said. "What do you think of your granddaughter?"

Mom teared-up. "She's beautiful. Absolutely beautiful."

"You definitely married up," Dad joked. He leaned down and kissed the baby. "Do you want Emily to come home with us?"

"That would be helpful," I said. "I'm gonna hang out here for a few hours then go home to change and come back." I turned to Emily. "Behave, and don't forget to feed your puppy."

"I will," Emily said, breaking eye contact.

Everyone was so happy about the baby, but it was clear something was going on with Emily. "What's wrong baby?"

"Nothing," she said, wiping her eyes. A moment later tears started to fall.

"Oh my gosh," Annie said. "Today's your actual birthday?" Emily nodded, not able to stop her tears. "Oh baby, come here."

Emily fell into Annie's free arm. I felt like someone punched me in the gut. I was the world's worst dad. Although we had given Emily presents working up to her birthday, we forgot her actual birthday. I joined in the group hug.

"Once we get settled back home," I said, "you and me will go fishing again. This time we'll go up to Buggs Island

Lake okay?" Emily perked up and smiled. I placed both my arms on her shoulders so she faced me. I nodded over towards the baby and whispered, "Don't tell Addison, but you're always gonna be my best first baby."

I got a hug and she said, "I love you, Daddy."

An hour later I wheeled my mom outside with Emily. The news camera crews were gone. A new story must have tugged on their ADHD mindset. Across the parking lot, JT lifted Brooke into the back seat of his SUV. Sally waved from the passenger seat. Dad pulled his truck around. The two of us lifted Mom into the passenger seat. She winced but didn't complain.

I kissed Emily and Mom before turning to my dad who was back in the driver's seat. "You got precious cargo here old man, so be careful."

"Roger that."

JT drove passed us and beeped his horn. A few moments later Dad pulled away, leaving me alone in the parking lot. It was now just a hospital again, and I wanted to take Annie and Addison home. My cell phone rang. It was an unknown caller.

"Drake?"

"Where you at?"

"Hospital. Annie gave birth to a girl last night."

"That's such great news. Go be with your family and call me later. We can talk then—"

"No, what's up?"

"You sure that you have time?"

"I do."

"Jeb Lawson's still missing."

"FBI will find him, right?"

"I'm losing confidence by the minute. The Dismal Swamp is thousands of acres. I have ancestors that were runaway slaves called Maroons who used to hide out there because it was so dense. They built entire communities in the Dismal Swamp and no one could ever find them."

"Yeah, but with today's drone technology-"

"Swamp is too dense."

"Even with infrared?"

"You know how much wildlife is in there? It would light up any infrared scanner like it was a Fourth of July fireworks display. Jeb and his brother had lots of money backing them. For all we know he could have another underground bunker hidden deep in the swamp somewhere with ten years worth of survival food. Add in a water filter and the guy is as good as gone."

"Have you been able to follow any money trails?"

"Turns out Jeb Lawson's dad used to be a limo driver for Gaspar Schultz back in the seventies whenever he was in D.C. on business. There's definitely a family connection."

"I know Schultz is an evil globalist who's involved in a ton of nasty things, but do you think he's sick enough to be into something as sinister as child abductions and sex trafficking?"

Without pausing Drake said, "Yes."

"You're that sure?"

"Two hours after we left the site the cabin was destroyed using a suicide drone."

"Are you kidding me? Was anyone hurt?"

"One of the FBI agents received a minor injury, and a lot of the evidence was destroyed. The drone was a high-end military grade. Only someone like Schultz could pull this off."

"What the-"

"Oh, it gets worse. Soon after the cabin was destroyed, we got a coded message from someone I believe was affiliated with Schultz. We haven't decoded it yet, but I believe it's going to give us a lead to help find Jeb Lawson."

"Wait, I'm confused. Schultz has the Lawson brothers on payroll, destroys their cabin, and then contacts you with a possible lead to catch his employee?"

"Doesn't sound so strange if you play it out, Brandon. Jeb's brother is dead and his network's destroyed. He's compromised and if he, theoretically, goes off the deep end then he goes from being an asset to a liability for Schultz."

"What's the message you guys were sent?"

"Not sure yet. Trying to decipher what it means. My hope is it will show us where Lawson's hiding out. Stay tuned."

Back inside the hospital Annie was asleep. I scribbled a note letting her know I was heading home to check on the farm and would be back shortly. Through the glassed nursery window, I could see Addison sleeping. She was wrapped in a cocoon type blanket with her pink beanie cap on. Her lips were puckered like she had just sucked on a lemon. I was in love. I didn't know if it was exhaustion, the birth of my daughter, Brooke being rescued, or a combination of the three, but the world seemed less evil. I knew the moment would pass, but I enjoyed the optimistic feeling. There would someday be a day with no more tears, no more sorrow, and no more death.

Back at the farm I drove the property checking on the herd. I couldn't wait to take my new daughter in the cab of a tractor and drive her around the property. Inside the house, I set the coffee and jumped in the shower. The hot water felt good against my sore back from sleeping in the hospital recliner. I stayed in the shower until it ran out of hot water. After a change of clothes and a cup of coffee I found my cell phone in a mess of colors. I forgot it was on silent mode. Green lights signifying missed calls were interspersed with multicolored texts. I scrolled through the texts first. Drake sent three which all said to call him. The phone calls and voicemails were also my friend. I dialed his cell and left it on speakerphone.

"Brandon, where've you been?"

"I was in the shower. What's wrong?"

"Where you at?"

"Home."

"We cracked the code that was sent to us."

"And?"

"And it was a number allowing us to geolocate a burner cell phone we believe Jeb Lawson has on him."

"And?"

"And it was heading towards you but went dark about a mile north." Drake inhaled before he spoke next. "I think he's coming for you."

"For me?" I said, walking into my closet. I placed the phone down so I could rummage through the sea chest in my closet.

"Guy is off his rocker with grief over his brother's death and probably wants to exact revenge on you," Drake said. "I sent a message to the sheriff's office to get someone over to your place."

Images of a firefight on my property from the past came rushing back. During that nightmare my home was almost destroyed, and both me, Annie, and my dad were almost killed.

"Brandon, you still there?"

"Yeah," I said, loading a Glock 19 and stuffing it into a Kydex holster.

"Grab your nearest gun, lock all your doors, and-"

"Wait," I said, picking up the phone. "Where did you say Jeb Lawson's signal went dark?"

"About a mile north of you. I think he may have been

using a mapping function to locate you and either destroyed the phone or shut it down once he got close."

Suddenly I realized who lived a mile north of me. I grabbed my keys and ran out the door. "Drake, he's not coming for me," I shouted. "Sally and Brooke Eldridge live just north of me."

EIGHTEEN

I HUNG UP ON DRAKE AND JUMPED INTO MY TRUCK. I TORE out of the driveway and realized the glass-packed mufflers would sound like cannons announcing my arrival at the Eldridge property. Stealth was not going to be an option. A Sheriff's cruiser with lights blazing passed by heading towards my property. I didn't have time to turn around and flag him down. What seemed like seconds later, I turned onto the gravel driveway that led to Sally Eldridge's small ranch home. I dropped Hazel into second gear and gunned the truck down the first half of the driveway to pick up as much momentum as possible before popping it into neutral. This would let the truck cruise the remainder of the way quiet. A moment later I realized stealth wasn't needed. An old sedan was parked next to JT's SUV. On the elevated side porch stood Jeb Lawson. He held a shotgun and looked like he was about to kick in the side door. He turned when he saw my truck.

I dropped it back into second gear and gunned the 6.4-liter engine. Hazel sounded like a roaring dragon. This would be the last time I'd hear her engine rumble. Jeb turned and fired off a round of buckshot at me which at this distance was like pebbles hitting Hazel's grill. I kept driving with the pedal pressed to the floor. It was too late to put on a seatbelt. A moment later the windshield splintered from a second blast from the shotgun. I didn't care. Hazel would hold together long enough to do her final job. The engine and tachometer screamed. I shifted into third gear. With a crunch of metal and wood Hazel burst through the pressure treated four-by-four posts like they were matchsticks. My head hit something, and a piece of wood came through the passenger's side of the windshield. I kept my foot on the gas pushing through the wreckage into the sloped backyard where the weight and momentum of the truck carried me down towards a small river. I let go of the steering wheel and was tossed about the truck cab like popcorn. At one point I thought the truck would flip but she kept her course. A moment later the front end of the truck rested in the river with steam pouring out from the radiator. My eyesight blurred from the blood. A quick check revealed a gash on my forehead, sore spots all over, but nothing seemed broken.

The driver's door wouldn't open, and neither would the passenger's. I kicked out the remainder of the windshield and crawled out over the hood cutting my stomach on shards of glass in the process. Slithering off the hood I fell into the river. The water washed the blood away and woke me with a cold snap. Through the steam from the truck's hood I could see a hazy picture of the side of the Eldridge house. I had ripped the entire side porch off from the house. Wood was scattered about the back yard, but Jeb was nowhere in sight. JT was crawling out a back window and waving one of his arms back and forth as if to warn me of something.

Suddenly, the cab of the truck exploded with glass from

the back window. Jeb rose up from the bed of the truck covered in blood. He had fallen into the back of the pickup when I tore off the porch. He was surrounded by busted timbers and kept blasting the cab where I had been seconds earlier. Jeb stopped firing, looked inside for my body. While he did this I felt around and found the Kydex holster was still clipped on my belt. Jeb saw me and swung the shotgun in my direction. He racked the slide, launching a spent plastic cartridge of buckshot into Hazel's bed. At this range that rifle would remove my head from my shoulders. I started to remove the gun but was slowed down with my arm underwater. Images of Smith Mountain Lake and the Dismal Swamp flooded my mind as a reminder of where I was.

I dropped below the water and moved to the left. It sounded like someone dropped a boulder next to my head as water exploded where I had just been. Pain seared my shoulder and face from the buckshot. It was like getting stung by a thousand bees. I continued to move to the left as another round went off nearby. The explosion of water pushed me aside to where the river current picked me up. If I could stay underwater, the river would carry me around a bend and out of range. An image of Brooke Eldridge came to mind as a reminder that I couldn't flee. I pushed off the bottom and rose up out of the water gun drawn. Jeb had the shotgun pointed to where I had just been. I had no idea if my gun would fire after being submerged. If not, then I was going to die a painful death.

I pulled the trigger and the sound of a nine-millimeter round went off followed by another then another. I hit center mass each time. Jeb convulsed in the back of the truck before collapsing after the fourth round hit him. I half-swam half-walked over to shore keeping my gun pointed towards the slumped figure laying on the roof of the truck. Blood soaked through a beige shirt down into the cab of the truck revealing that he wore no body armor this time. Jeb Lawson was dead.

I pulled the shotgun from the lifeless hands before wading back into the river. The water was a balm to the pain that seared my shoulder and face. I felt around and everything was still intact. Once again, the water was the saving factor in my life. Being underwater had softened the blow of the buckshot to the point where I only had superficial wounds, but I was still nervous to go look in the truck mirror to see the extent of the damage. Someone jumped into the river and a moment later JT pulled me out of the water. I could tell by the grin on his face my wounds weren't life-threatening.

"You're one crazy redneck, you know that?"

"He shot my truck," I mumbled, trying to be funny and fend off going into shock.

"Let's get you topside."

Within minutes I had an icepack held to the side of my face and a clean towel against my forehead. Not long after, Sally's driveway was filled with police, sheriff, and EMT's.

Sally was in tears. "Oh Brandon, I'm so sorry-"

I held up a shaking hand. "Don't you dare apologize for an evil act someone else did. Where's Brooke?"

"She's asleep. Her bedroom's down the other end of the house and I had a fan going for white noise to help her sleep. Jeb had just come on the porch when you showed up."

"Go be with her and don't let her outside," I said. "The last thing we need is her finding out what just happened. It would traumatize her further." I felt in my back pocket and pulled out my second water-logged cell phone. "Can someone call my wife and let her know I'm okay?"

"On it," JT said.

Four police officers escorted two EMT's as they struggled to push a gurney up the hill from the backyard. I was surprised Jeb's body wasn't covered over. As they crested the hill onto the gravel driveway, I noticed his chest moving up and down.

"He's alive?"

"Barely," an elderly male EMT said. "Move out of the way. We gotta get him out of here."

Several law enforcement officers moved, but they didn't seem to have a sense of urgency. It was as if they didn't care if Jeb Lawson was given proper medical treatment or not. The EMT repeated himself and finally got Jeb loaded into a waiting ambulance. A part of me was sad that Jeb Lawson survived. Another part was relieved I didn't take his life, and another part of me realized that while there was breath in his lungs there was still a chance that the wretched man could turn to God. I doubted it would happen, but only the Almighty knew. Standing beside me, JT recapped the events to a female officer.

"Jeb was screaming for Brooke. Saying she belonged to him. The guy's obsessed. I have no idea how he tracked us here."

"I've never seen anything like this," the officer said.

JT thumbed towards me. "Then this crazy dude comes out of nowhere."

The officer turned to me. "How'd you happen to be here?"

I didn't know if I should bring up Drake's name. Instead, what I said was, "I live down the street and stopped by on the way back to the hospital where I was going to see my newborn daughter."

A few minutes later the EMT's transported me in a second ambulance to the hospital. I would have tried to drive myself, but my truck was ruined, and I was dizzy from hitting my head, and my shoulder and face were sore from the buckshot. Had I not been underwater when Jeb fired the shotgun, I would have had more than just sting marks. Inside the ambulance the adrenaline from the fight seemed to drain away. I wanted nothing more than to shut my eyes, but the annoying EMT kept telling me to keep them open. I knew it was a safety precaution in case I had a concussion.

What seemed like minutes later the ambulance came to a stop. I remember the legs extending on the gurney and leaving the warm ambulance into the cool outside air. They delivered me somewhere into the emergency room. A familiar annoying voice started to ask me questions, but I didn't answer. I wanted just to sleep. Whoever it was, slapped me in the face. I opened my eyes to see Jamie standing next to me. She had a horrified expression on her face, like I had just done something really stupid. I started to wonder if I had.

"You don't do anything small do you, Brandon?"

"It wasn't my fault," I said in a hoarse voice.

She looked under a bandage on my forehead. "Oh, your poor wife."

"What are you doing in the ER?"

"I heard you were coming in an ambulance and rushed down here thinking you had nothing more than a broken fingernail." She readjusted the bandage. "You're gonna need stitches, but you'll live."

She proceeded to check my vitals, stuck a pen light into my eyes which felt like a laser beam. Before Jamie left, she gave instructions to an orderly to take me for an x-ray. On the way back from the x-ray I passed by a double door entrance with a sign which read, "Operating Room". A South Boston Police officer stood guard outside the doors. Jeb Lawson was inside that room being operated on. Some surgeon was removing bullets I had lodged in his body. I needed to let go of the anger I had towards the evil man and the wicked practice he dealt in. My dad once told me that holding on to anger and bitterness was like drinking a cup of poison and hoping the other person would get sick. It was in God's hands.

I was placed back in a random room somewhere in the ER. An orderly handed me some hospital scrubs so I could get out of my damp clothes. I went into the hallway bathroom to get changed. In the mirror I had a bandage around my head which looked like a melted marshmallow. There was a red spot of blood in the bandage over my left eye where I hit my head. The right side of my face was pockmarked where the buckshot hit but didn't penetrate the skin. It just looked like I had an allergic reaction to some shellfish. There were splotches of blood mixed in my beard. I ran my fingers through and dug out a single buckshot just under the skin near my jaw. It felt like a pressure valve was released on my face. My shoulder was red from buckshot, but overall, I was in one piece. I looked up at the ceiling and thanked God for yet another miracle.

When I came back into the room, Annie sat in a chair next to the bed. She had on a bathrobe. I could tell she had been crying. I didn't say anything and proceeded to crawl into the bed and pulled the blanket up to my chin.

"You're going to be the death of me," she said.

"Sorry."

"Do you know how worried I've been?"

"Sorry."

"Is that all you have to say?"

I gave her a goofy grin which I knew was exacerbated by the horrible bandage and my swollen face. "You realize we're all alone in a private room," I said. "Wanna make-out?"

She put her hand to her mouth to stifle a laugh. A moment later she shuffled over to the bed and crawled in next to me. I lifted the thin blanket and cradled the woman I loved.

"How you feeling?" I asked.

"Better than you look."

"How's Addison?"

"She said her first words already."

"Oh really," I said, preparing for a punchline. "And they were?"

"That she wants her dad alive long enough to see her get married."

"Sorry for ruining your Hallmark Channel birth experience. We can try again in nine to twelve months."

"Just how many more children do you want?"

"I'd like to field my own softball team."

"That's not funny, Brandon."

EPILOGUE

THE NEXT TWENTY-FOUR HOURS WERE AN EMOTIONAL roller coaster ride. One moment I was full of joy seeing my wife and newborn daughter, and the next, I fielded long phone calls from law enforcement needing more details on the case. FBI, now aware of the Darren Eldridge-Jeb Lawson computer connection, uncovered a bank transaction for two thousand dollars between the two men. Initial thoughts were Lawson obtained personal information on Sandy and Brooke from Darren Eldridge in exchange for money. Darren, a drunk who was heavily in debt to local bookies, used the money to pay down what he owed.

After seeing the picture of Brooke, Jeb Lawson became obsessed and stalked her family from the shadows online. He spent months planning out Brooke's kidnapping at the homeschool convention. During this time, he encouraged no less than a dozen registered, and unregistered, pedophile sex offenders in the Richmond area to try to hit the *target-rich* convention. He did this from different websites using different aliases. Only one man, William Jeffers, was baited into trying, which created the perfect diversion for Jeb to grab Brooke. The timing of Darren Eldridge's death also triggered law enforcement to order his body to be exhumed, and a posthumous autopsy conducted to see if it was murder rather than natural causes. If Jeb Lawson was a protégé of Gaspar Schultz then he was trained to leave no trails.

Two days later I carried my newborn daughter into her home for the first time. Annie came in behind me looking like she'd never had a baby. A text appeared on my new cell phone from Drake. He said to call him when I had a minute. I was nervous it was more bad news, and waited until both Annie and the baby were resting and Emily was busy with schoolwork before calling him back.

"What's up?"

"Jeb Lawson's dead."

My heart sank. As much as I loathed the man I did not like the fact that I took his life. "From the gunshot wounds?"

"Poison," Drake said. "Lawson had enough poison injected into him to kill an elephant."

"What?"

"Someone wanted to make sure the canary didn't sing. The officer assigned to the room is being interviewed and video surveillance is being reviewed, but I'm not optimistic. There are poisons which have a delayed reaction and could have been given to him before an officer showed up. Could have even been given to him in the ambulance for all we know."

"Gaspar Schultz?" I said.

"I would assume one of his minions."

"So we did the dirty work for Schultz by finding his rogue employee just so he could dispose of him."

"Yup. I'm a fool for not realizing this. Just thought you'd want to know."

"I appreciate it."

"Did you get my present for Addison?"

"Hold on," I said, walking into the kitchen. Next to Emily was a pile of mail. Two packages were mixed in. One was from the company Annie ordered vitamins from. The other was addressed to "the newest Hall" with no return address. "I'm opening it now," I said.

Drake giggled on the other end of the phone like a schoolboy. The package was an 8x10 picture of Drake. Just a picture of him in a fancy three-piece suit with his hands holding the lapels like he was some old time vaudeville performer. The picture was signed like it was from a celebrity.

I read it out loud. "Dear Addison, stay motivated." I had to laugh as well. The man was so over-the-top that it was self-deprecating. It wasn't until I got off the phone that I found a $500 check attached to the back of the picture labeled, *For Addison's college fund.*

Fescue came running over the porch with something in her mouth. I thought it might be a rodent but couldn't make it out as she slammed the creature from side to side as if to shake it to death.

"Fescue, come here," I said, stepping onto the porch. She understood her name, but like most females in my life she ignored me. For the next two minutes I chased her around the front yard. I must have looked like an idiot but at this point it was personal. Man against beast in a battle of willpower. Finally, I lunged at the dog and grabbed her by the scruff of the neck. What was in her mouth wasn't a squirrel or rabbit, but Emily's stuffed teddy bear from the homeschool convention. The head was half decapitated, and it was missing an arm and opposite leg. I pried the teddy bear from her mouth and Fescue growled like I had taken food from her.

"Sorry young lady, but-"

Something sparkled from inside the stuffing in the bear's neck. I reached in and pulled out what looked like a nickel-sized microchip. On the backside it had a hearing aid sized battery attached to it. This was the same teddy bear Brooke Eldridge held throughout her recovery. This was how Jeb Lawson tracked her and how he could track other potential future targets as well. I took a picture of it and sent it off to Drake.

The sound of off-road tires against gravel in the driveway reminded me of the way my truck used to sound, but this was smoother than the noise Hazel made. Bubba D'Angelo drove up in a truck that looked almost identical to Hazel. Bubba was a friend and the best auto body guy in Halifax County. It took me a moment to realize the truck he drove was Hazel. However, the faded blue paint was brand new. She had new tires and shiny chrome rims as well.

Bubba smiled as he shut off the truck. "What do you think?"

"What do I think?" I repeated. "I'm in love." I looked inside the cab. You could have eaten off the floor. "I thought she wasn't salvageable?"

"JT insisted," he said, handing me the keys. "And paid my staff to work around the clock to get her done so quick."

When I started her up the truck sounded like a fine-tuned musical instrument. One of Bubba's employees pulled up in another truck to drive him back to the shop. I didn't know what to say. Instead I hugged him.

Sitting in the new dark brown leather seats of the truck I thought back over the craziness of the past month. My wife and both my children were safe and healthy. Mom was recovering. Brooke Eldridge was home and recovering. Even my truck was healthy. I prayed that my family was entering a season of peace on the farm. However, I knew that beyond the fence line of the property was a world where evil still existed. Throughout history this evil took on names which now included Gaspar Schultz. All of whom served the god of this world, and this evil did not sleep.

It seemed over the past few years I had been fighting a proxy war with Gaspar Schultz through his surrogates. The first time ended in a shootout with an anarchist group he funded. This time was in a shootout with someone who worked directly for him. We seemed to be in a morbid dance, and our concentric circles were getting closer to intersecting.

NOTE FROM THE AUTHOR

Out of the eight books I've authored, *The Dismal Swamp* may be the most important story I've written. Ironically, it was by far the least enjoyable to research and write. Although many of the scenarios, and antagonists, in my other novels had realistic components to them, at the end of the day they were still fiction. *The Dismal Swamp's* setting may have been fiction, but the human traffickers in it are all too real. How evil of this sort exists today is beyond upsetting. What's nearly as disturbing is how desensitized our culture has become to it. After researching the world of human trafficking, I can only conclude that now, more than ever, our world is in dire need of a Savior.

John Theo Jr.

STATISTICS ON HUMAN TRAFFICKING

Taken from do www.dosomething.org

Trafficking primarily involves exploitation which comes in many forms, including: forcing victims into prostitution, subjecting victims to slavery or involuntary servitude and compelling victims to commit sex acts for the purpose of creating pornography.

According to some estimates, approximately 80% of trafficking involves sexual exploitation, and 19% involves labor exploitation.

According to the U.S. State Department, 600,000 to 800,000 people are trafficked across international borders every year, of which 80% are female and half are children.

The average age a teen enters the sex trade in the United States is 12 to 14-year-old. Many victims are runaway girls who were sexually abused as children.

Between 14,500 and 17,500 people are trafficked into the U.S. each year.

Human trafficking is the third largest international crime industry (behind illegal drugs and arms trafficking). It reportedly generates a profit of $32 billion every year. Of that number, $15.5 billion is made in industrialized countries.

There are approximately 20 to 30 million slaves in the world today.

TAKE A LOOK AT BENEATH DC
A BRANDON HALL MYSTERY 3

Brandon Hall is back in a mesmerizing, fast-paced mystery that reveals secrets at every turn.

Once again, cattle farmer and part time private investigator Brandon Hall, is drawn into a case well above his pay grade. While working on a contract job in Washington DC, Brandon's path crosses that of his government friend Roger Drake. Brandon uncovers a piece of evidence tied to one of Drake's cases and agrees to join his team for this one job.

Together, they uncover a world even more treacherous than the swamp known as Washington DC. The secret globalist organization known as Gehenna is meeting for the first time in a decade. Unhappy with the last election, Gehenna plans a false flag attack on US soil in an attempt to reboot, and redirect, the United States. Brandon, along with Drake's team, must find the hidden location of the group, and stop them at all costs.

In this third chapter of the series, Brandon finally comes face-to-face with Gaspar Schultz, the vile leader of the group responsible for the string of deadly cases he has worked on.

PURCHASE NOW!

ABOUT THE AUTHOR

John Theo Jr. received a bachelor's degree in psychology from Salem State University, and an M.F.A. in Creative Writing from Pine Manor College in Chestnut Hill, Massachusetts. For almost two decades his diverse writing portfolio included roles as a movie critic, a magazine freelance writer, and a college professor where he taught screenwriting.

John grew up in the suburbs north of Boston where much of his youth was spent buried under stacks of comic books. He latched onto any story involving far off places and fantastical characters. Years later he realized the novels and movies that impacted him on the deepest level were ones with a spiritual component. In hindsight, he realized that his youthful obsession with these stories was, in fact, a longing for the Divine.

Today, John Theo Jr. writes novels from a Christian perspective. Like the stories of his youth, John enjoys tales with an otherworldly component to them as well as a good measure of action, adventure, and romance.

READ MORE ABOUT JOHN THEO JR. HERE

Made in the USA
Columbia, SC
08 July 2020

13495165R00140